CAPTIVE WITNESS

by
Carolyn Keene

Illustrated by
Paul Frame

WANDERER BOOKS
Published by Simon & Schuster, New York

Manufactured in the United States of America
10 9 8 7 6 5 4 3 2

NANCY DREW and NANCY DREW MYSTERY STORIES
are trademarks of Stratemeyer Syndicate,
registered in the United States Patent
and Trademark Office
WANDERER and colophon are trademarks of Simon & Schuster

Library of Congress Cataloging in Publication Data

Keene, Carolyn.
Captive witness.

(Nancy Drew mystery stories/Carolyn Keene; no.64)
Summary: Trouble plagues a student tour through
Europe as Nancy becomes involved in a plot to smuggle
refugee children across the Austrian border from
Eastern Europe.
[1. Mystery and detective stories.   2. Refugees—
Fiction.   3. Austria—Fiction]   I. Frame, Paul,
ill.   II. Title.   III. Series: Keene, Carolyn.
Nancy Drew mystery stories; no. 64.
PZ7.K23   Nan, no. 64   [Fic]   81-11414
ISBN 0-671-42360-6   AACR2
ISBN 0-671-42361-4 (pbk.)

Contents

1   *Airport Trouble*   7

2   *The Shaking Bus*   19

3   *The Mozart Lecture*   29

4   *Mysterious Interference*   40

5   *An Unpleasant Invitation*   50

6   *Kidnapped!*   57

7   *Hazardous Ride*   63

8   *Danger in the Alps*   69

9   *The Alpine Prison*   77

10   *Amphibian on Wheels*   85

11   *Wild-Goose Chase*   95

12   *Captive Witness*   105

13   *The Stricken Messenger*   112

14   *The Terrible Truth*   120

15   *Perilous Plan*   130

16   *The Shoppers' Ploy*   138

17   *Freedom Props*   144

18   *A Hero Arrives*   155

19   *Across the Frontier*   169

20   *Herr Gutterman Unmasked*   179

1

Airport Trouble

Nancy Drew brushed a strand of titian hair out of her eyes and patted it back into place as she stood in the Munich, Germany, airline terminal reading a cablegram.

NANCY DREW
C/O EMERSON COLLEGE AUSTRIAN TOUR
PAN AMERICAN AIRWAYS
MUNICH.
DEAR NANCY:
HAVE INTERESTING AND URGENT CASE RE FILM STOLEN FROM VIENNA FESTIVAL OFFICE. CALL ME IMMEDIATELY.

LOVE,
DAD

As he had so often, Carson Drew was calling on the detective skills of his eighteen-year-old daughter on behalf of one of his legal clients. This time, by coincidence, the mystery involved the final destination of Nancy's tour group, the city of Vienna.

The trip was being sponsored by Emerson College which her special friend, Ned Nickerson, attended along with two other freshmen who frequently dated Nancy's closest companions, Bess Marvin and George Fayne. As soon as the girls heard about the Austrian tour, they arranged to join it.

"I hope you're holding good news," Ned said, as he joined Nancy on the edge of a crowd of happy students milling around Professor Raymond Bagley, the college tour leader.

Ned was Nancy's most ardent admirer and she couldn't resist teasing in reply. "Well, I don't know if you'll think it's good news or not, but Dad's just assigned me to another case and I may have to leave the tour for a few days."

Ned groaned. "Not another mystery?" Then he brightened. "On the other hand, maybe I can go with you on this one?"

Before Nancy could answer, Dr. Bagley's voice was heard. "All right. Everybody here? Anybody missing, speak up." The professor with his shock of unruly brown hair and his oversize, brown-rimmed glasses gave the appearance of a happy owl.

He had no trouble seeing everyone in his group since he was almost six feet, six inches tall, though slightly stooped from more than twenty years spent leaning down trying to hear what was going on in his classroom.

Nancy waved to get Professor Bagley's attention. "Two of them are missing, sir, as usual," she called, her blue eyes twinkling.

"Oh, no, not again!" moaned her girlfriend, slim, attractive George Fayne. She clutched her short, dark hair in mock despair. "Wait. Don't tell me," she said. "Let me guess. I see it all in my crystal ball. There's this couple. It's—" She covered her eyes with one hand and waved the fingers of the other hand in pretended excitement. "It's Bess Marvin! And Dave Evans! They are entering a snack bar. They have disappeared into a snack bar. They won't come out!"

"Correct." The girl detective laughed. "Your pretty cousin with the weakness for food, and her constant companion with a weakness for Bess."

"All right," called the professor, "let's all grab our bags and those of our two missing friends and we'll find the bus. It should be in this area over here."

But before Dr. Bagley could move, he was confronted by a big, hard-faced man in a porter's uniform. He bowed, clicked his heels, and picked up the tour leader's suitcases and his small musette bag which still bore the government initials, very faintly—U.S.

"Permit me, sir," the porter said with a slight accent. "Permit me, Herr Professor Bagley."

The professor adjusted his glasses and stared.

Ned Nickerson smiled. "Well, Professor Bagley," he said, "we all knew you had an outstanding international reputation as an art and music expert but here's the proof. Everybody knows you."

But the usually affable teacher didn't smile. Instead, he took a step toward the porter and extended his long arms. "See here," he said sharply. "Give me that luggage. I thank you for your courtesy but I'll carry my own bags, if you don't mind."

The porter attempted to smile reassuringly but his hard features couldn't make the effort. Instead, he took a few steps back, bowed, and clicked his heels again. "*Nein, nein,*" he protested. "I'll take care of everything." He walked away very rapidly toward the door leading to the taxis.

"Come back here," called the professor.

"*Ja*, I will meet you on the other side," the porter shouted over his shoulder as he threw the bags on a hand truck and began pushing it away at a fast trot.

Professor Bagley waved his arms. "What does he mean, 'the other side'? The tour bus area is in the *opposite* direction. What is he doing?"

"I think, sir," said Nancy, moving quickly to Professor Bagley's side, "that he's stealing your bags."

"Oh, no," Ned declared. "He just *thinks* he's stealing them. Burt!" He motioned to the short, but powerfully built, Burt Eddleton who was George's beau. Both boys were on the Emerson College football team and their quick reactions showed why. They zigzagged their way through the crowd, streaking after the rapidly disappearing porter.

Both Nancy and George were close on the boys' heels—too close for George because as Ned and Burt left the ground and attempted to hurdle a pile of suitcases, they became entangled and went flying over the luggage with George sailing right over the top of them.

Nancy, narrowly averting the pileup, saw the porter dash out the doors toward the lines of taxis, buses, and private cars. As luck would have it, he collided with another hand truck which delayed him long enough for Nancy to veer off and go through a set of doors that brought her out on the sidewalk a hundred feet ahead of him.

As the man ran toward her, pushing the truck, he suddenly looked stunned and angry to find Nancy blocking his path.

"Get out of the way, girl, or I'll hurt you!" he snarled.

Nancy did not budge, though. "Just drop those

suitcases," she said evenly. "Drop them on the ground and I'll let you go."

The man, who was well over six feet tall, heavyset with large, muscular arms, couldn't believe his ears. "*You?*" he sputtered. "*You* will let *me* go? You insignificant little creature. You stupid girl. I will crush you like a bug!"

Without further warning, he charged at the girl detective, the angle of his attack leaving her little choice but to outrun him or jump into the speeding traffic.

Instinctively, Nancy made her move. She leaped high, grabbed a projecting pipe, swung her feet up and over the oncoming car and dropped them solidly on the man's right shoulder.

The impact broke her hold and she was thrown to the ground but managed to scramble quickly to her feet. Her opponent wasn't as lucky or skilled, much less prepared for an eighteen-year-old girl capable of such acrobatic feats of strength. As a result, when Nancy's feet hit his shoulder he tripped off balance. The force of the impact spun him around. He lost his hold on the cart and went crashing into the wall.

Nancy quickly grabbed the professor's bags, threw them behind her and assumed a defensive judo position. The porter, bleeding from a cut on the head, struggled to his feet and was about to attack when he heard the cries of Nancy's friends in hot pursuit.

Realizing he could not win, he pointed a thick finger at the girl detective. "You get in our way again, Nancy Drew, and I promise you, I will get you. I will take care of you, *myself!*"

Suddenly, the man was gone. He had vaulted a railing and leaped into a black sedan which moved off so quickly that Nancy had no time to check the license plate.

Ned ran up, limping from his fall, and took her by the shoulders. "Are you all right, Nancy?"

She looked up at him, smiling, but still panting from her struggle with the "porter." She nodded, "Oh, sure, Ned. I'm okay. But he *escaped.*" Her voice was filled with disappointment.

"It's just as well," George gasped. "He looked as if it would take an army to capture him. Good riddance."

Ned and Burt took the suitcases and they all walked back toward the waiting room. Professor Bagley, who could not move too fast because of a leg wound received during his army service, came up to them, casual and smiling.

"I can't thank you enough," he said, when told of Nancy's successful confrontation with the would-be thief. "You're a wonder, Nancy. Do you think he had time to open the bags and take anything?"

"Impossible," she said. "I had my eyes on him every inch of the way and, as you can see, the straps are all in place."

But Nancy's detective instincts were beginning to stir as she watched Professor Bagley's almost too casual attitude toward the threatened theft. "What in the world did that man think you were carrying in your luggage?" Nancy asked.

The professor simply laughed. "Beats me. Maybe he wears size fourteen double A, too. I heard there were one or two other people in the world with feet that size."

For the first time since she had known Professor Bagley, the girl detective realized he was skirting the truth. He wasn't lying. He just wasn't saying much. There is something special in his luggage, she decided—something he doesn't want anyone to know about. Yet how could he be so calm when it was almost stolen?

Once aboard the tour bus, however, the attempted theft was pushed into the back of Nancy's mind. She stopped at the wheelchair which occupied a special area in the front of the bus and spoke with the occupant, a handsome young man named Eric Nagy. Eric was an Emerson student who, though in his early twenties, had just entered college. Months before the tour, he had been involved in an auto accident which left him paralyzed from the waist down. He was blond, with a wide jaw, prominent cheekbones, and soft hazel eyes which Bess called "hauntingly poetic." Eric's parents had come from Hungary but he had been born in River Heights.

"Hi, everybody! Did you miss us?" Bess grinned. A chorus of shouts, groans, and whistles greeted the arrival of the pretty, blond girl and her friend, Dave Evans.

Nancy quickly motioned for Bess to sit beside her. "You missed all the excitement," Nancy told her as the bus started off. She recounted the attempted theft of the professor's bags.

"Wow!" Bess exclaimed, "and the guy really said he was going to get you?"

"Oh," Nancy scoffed, "I'm not worried about myself."

"But what about Professor Bagley?" Bess answered. "He may be famous, but he's not rich. Why would a thief single him out?"

"I don't know," Nancy said. "I do have this gnawing feeling, though, that the professor is in danger."

"Oh, I hope not." Bess sighed. "I mean, what's going to happen to our beautiful, peaceful trip? After all the plans we've made and—"

"Shhh," Nancy said. "Did you hear that?"

They both listened. A strange thumping and bumping noise seemed to be coming from the bottom of the bus. It continued for five minutes. Finally, Bess said, "I'm going to tell the driver." Marching up to the front of the bus, she reported the noise, listened to his explanation, and returned to her seat.

"He said it was nothing," Bess informed her friend.

"Nothing? It sounded as if the bus were ready to fall apart."

"Well, I don't hear it now," Bess said. Suddenly, however, the noise erupted again. "This is ridiculous," she remarked. "Nancy, why don't you talk to the driver this time since I couldn't get anywhere?"

Nancy got up and confronted the man. His manner was short, rude, and irritated.

"It is nothing but a loose tool bouncing around in the luggage compartment. If the *Fräuleins* ever expect to get to Salzburg, they must stop annoying me with such stupid questions."

Nancy returned and looked at Bess. "There is no noise. Or, if there is, it is just a loose tool bouncing around in the luggage. Also, the *Fräuleins* have to stop annoying the bus driver, he says."

"What a grouch," Bess said. "Never mind. Look, we're pulling off the road for a rest stop."

When the bus rolled to a halt, everyone, except Nancy, exited toward the restaurant. She had felt her left shoelace snap and by the time she had fixed it, found herself alone. "I knew I should have worn loafers," she grumbled, leaving the bus to join the others. Then she stopped.

Thinking no one was watching, the driver had raised the hood of the engine and was disconnecting

17

a large part. He looked around furtively, then threw the part behind some nearby bushes, closed the hood, and headed for the restaurant.

Nancy felt her heartbeat step up. Their own driver was sabotaging the tour bus! Why?

2

The Shaking Bus

The driver, who was a wiry, sallow-faced man with pitted skin and dark eyes, wore a black cap to cover his almost totally bald head.

"Attention," he called in a rasping, somewhat high voice, as he came through the restaurant door. "Attention. I'm afraid there will be a little delay. The bus has broken down. They will have to send a new part out from Munich."

"How long will that take?" Professor Bagley asked.

"Not long," the driver said. "You can find accommodations at the hotel next door for the night. The part should be here by noon tomorrow."

"Tomorrow!" the professor cried. "Oh, see here,

19

that will throw our schedule off completely. What's wrong with the bus? Several of our students are excellent mechanics. Why not let them take a look?"

"No!" the driver shouted, his face suddenly burning with anger. "They cannot fix it. I myself am an expert mechanic. I know what I'm talking about. These are mere boys. They know nothing."

"Do you suppose this would help you repair your bus, Mr. Expert Mechanic?"

The bus driver whirled to see Nancy standing in the doorway holding an automobile part at eye level. The driver turned pale.

"I don't need a woman's help," he blustered. "The part will be here in the morning."

"What is it exactly?" Professor Bagley said, adjusting his spectacles and peering hard at the object in Nancy's hand.

"It's a distributor cap, sir," Nancy told him. "If you remove it from an engine, there's no way for the electricity to flow to the spark plugs. I just saw our driver take this distributor cap off the engine and throw it into the bushes."

"In that case, we'd better call the police," Professor Bagley said coldly, advancing toward the culprit. The driver, cornered, took a step toward the door, but Ned, Dave, and Burt were already blocking it. Before anyone could stop him, the man turned and dived through a window!

He hit the ground, rolled, and came up running.

"After him! Get him!" the professor cried as the students burst out the door to chase the man. Ned had almost caught up and was ready to make a flying tackle when he heard warning shouts and screams behind him. He turned just in time to see an ominous black sedan bearing down on him in almost complete silence.

The young collegian had stopped for only a fraction of a second, but the danger of his situation made everything suddenly appear to move in slow motion. He felt his leg muscles contract and expand as his body leaned and he threw his arms up and out in a spread-eagle dive, feeling the wind rush beneath him. The car barely missed him, and Ned crashed into a ditch where he rolled over twice before coming to a sitting position.

He was just in time to see the car slow down, the door on the passenger side swing open, and the bus driver leap in. The door closed silently and the phantom car disappeared swiftly over the horizon of a hill.

"Boy, oh, boy!" Dave yelled as he led the charge of young people forward to see if their friend was all right. "I thought he was going to hit you for sure, Ned."

Ned got up, limping and massaging his left knee. "Twice in one day on that leg." He groaned. "Once

21

in the airport and now here." He flexed his leg and then grinned. "It's okay. But did you hear that car?"

"No," Nancy said. "I couldn't hear anything."

"That's what I mean. No sound! The driver had to be going at least sixty when he passed me. Then he stopped about twenty feet away. And when that little rat-faced guy jumped in, that car zoomed off without so much as a whisper."

"Well, it's custom-made," Nancy commented. "It looked like a Daimler, a Mercedes, and half a dozen other cars combined."

"Anybody see the driver?" Bess asked.

"I did," Nancy said. "And guess who? The porter who tried to steal the luggage. I'll never forget that face."

As soon as she could, Nancy cornered the professor alone. "Dr. Bagley, do you know something that maybe I should know? I realize we're all your students right now, but I'm also a pretty good detective. How about it? What's going on?"

The professor studied his pipe, which had gone out as usual, and then he motioned her to come with him. "Let's go get some lunch, and I'll try to explain."

But once they were seated at the neat red-and-white checkered table in the rear, Dr. Bagley spun the conversation out slowly. Nancy waited, conquering her inner impatience while the professor

22

ordered them both a light lunch and exchanged small talk with the waitress dressed Bavarian peasant-style.

When the waitress finally left, Professor Bagley cleared his throat, hunched his shoulders, and peered down at Nancy with his friendly, educated-owl expression. "Nancy, what I'm going to tell you must be kept in the strictest confidence. The safety of ten helpless children depends on your silence."

The girl detective nodded, feeling the hairs along the back of her neck prickle.

"I'm very much afraid," the man began with a sigh, "that in trying to do a good turn for a band of unfortunate little orphans I have placed my entire student tour in the most awful danger."

Nancy waited to hear more but the professor lapsed into silence, thinking. The tension built quickly inside her, forcing her to speak. "What kind of danger, sir?"

The professor brought both hands down on the table in an expression of frustration. "That's the maddening part of it," he snorted. "I don't know! I don't know how desperate these people may be or what they may do. Right now they seem to be doing nothing more than delaying us. But as the zero hour draws nearer, who knows to what extremes of violence they may be driven?"

Once again the man became quiet, causing Nancy

to burst with curiosity. "Professor Bagley," she said, gathering courage, "do you realize you've told me absolutely nothing except that you have to help ten children and that our tour may be in danger?" Her eyes twinkled at him. "Believe it or not, I guessed that last part."

The tour leader stared at her, then broke into his characteristic soft chuckle. He shook his head. "The absentminded professor," he said. He ran his hand through his unruly hair. "You know, Nancy, you have the most charming way of telling a boring old teacher that he's being—well, boring!"

Nancy started to protest. "Oh, no, sir. I didn't mean that."

But Dr. Bagley waved his hand and smiled. "No, no, no. I understand. Of course, you didn't. All right, let me get to the point. I'll start at the beginning."

He cleared his throat. "I trust that you will keep what I'm about to tell you completely confidential."

"Of course," Nancy assured him.

"From time to time, I work for our intelligence unit."

"You mean you're a secret agent for the United States?" the young detective asked, prompting a nod from the professor.

"About a month ago, I was approached to help a refugee repatriation group. These people take care of anyone needing their assistance to leave any of the oppressed countries of Eastern Europe and come to the West, that is, to Western Europe and America.

"They asked me to use this tour as a cover to help them bring across the Austrian border ten orphaned children whose closest relatives have already defected. Most of them are living in France, England, or America.

"The children range in age from six to thirteen. Unfortunately, the communist government of their homeland refuses to see this as a nonpolitical undertaking to reunite orphans with their families. Instead, they say that the government will take care of the children, and any attempt to bring the orphans out of Eastern Europe will be viewed as kidnapping."

"If the government won't let them go," Nancy said, "what can you or the refugee group do?"

"Ah," said the professor, arching his brows and holding up one long forefinger as he so often did when teaching, "that's the catch. The children are somewhere in Hungary. They are being kept in hiding by an organization of dedicated people who have sworn to get them safely across the border into Austria."

"How?"

"Somehow. I don't know and I won't until I get to

Vienna. Then I'll be told how they plan to use me and Eric to get the job done."

"Eric?" repeated the young sleuth, incredulous. "You mean Eric Nagy?"

The tour leader nodded, then motioned to Eric who was seated several tables away. As the smiling young man rolled his wheelchair forward, the professor said, "Eric, I've let Nancy in on our mission. I'm sure you won't mind because she could be of great help to us. Anyway, she's such a good sleuth with a nose for clues that she would have figured it out all by herself within a day, at most."

"Oh, wait a minute, Dr. Bagley," Nancy said, blushing. "Nobody is that astute."

"I'm delighted to be associated with the beautiful Miss Drew," said Eric, smiling and looking very intently at Nancy, so intently that she felt herself blush more deeply and observed Ned, watching from across the room, shift uncomfortably in his chair.

The professor nodded and grinned. "Yes," he said, "I knew, somehow, you'd feel that way. But back to business. Nancy, Eric got into this because his parents were born in Hungary. His family has always been very active in helping others escape from behind the Iron Curtain. Eric is now carrying on the tradition."

As Dr. Bagley talked, Nancy's mind raced over

the possibilities, wondering how a middle-aged professor with a leg wounded in the war and a young man confined to a wheelchair could possibly help refugees escape. Didn't such attempts always involve a great deal of running, jumping, and physical exertion? But it would be bad manners to ask and realizing she didn't have all the facts, the girl listened and said nothing.

"It so happens," the professor continued, "that this particular mission involves someone very close to Eric—a thirteen-year-old cousin who is one of those ten children."

"Excuse me." They looked up and saw Ned standing uncomfortably, trying to smile. "I just wanted to say that we're running pretty late and we don't have a bus driver anymore and I'd like to volunteer to drive everyone to Salzburg." Ned's eyes flicked from Nancy to Eric and back to the professor.

Dr. Bagley smiled. "I appreciate your concern for the tour, Ned. Thank you. I'll accept your kind offer. And please pardon our rudeness in excluding everyone but I've got to discuss something confidential with Nancy."

Ned nodded and moved off uneasily, allowing Professor Bagley to return to their main subject.

"Now," he said, as he finished his coffee and started to prepare one of his numerous pipes which he could never keep lit, "I'd like to explain about the porter who tried to steal my luggage. You see, it was a ruse that backfired on me. I knew somebody was going to try stealing the luggage and I *wanted* him to."

"What?" Nancy gasped. But before the professor could elaborate, Bess Marvin burst in the door, her eyes almost popping with excitement.

"Nancy! Dr. Bagley! Hurry! The bus! The bus! Something's happening to it. I think it's going to explode!"

3

The Mozart Lecture

For the second time since their arrival at the rest area, the tour group rushed out of the restaurant in response to an emergency. They ran to within fifty feet of the bus where they stopped as the professor warned urgently: "Stand back!" From the interior of the bus they could hear a series of noises, a fierce crashing and banging.

"It sounds like some kind of animal is in there," Burt said.

"I think it's going to explode!" Bess cried, wringing her hands. "It is, isn't it? It's going to explode and nobody wants to tell me."

"Explode?" repeated the professor. "Why in the world would it explode?"

"Because maybe there's a bomb inside," Bess said, clutching the professor's arm. "Maybe that crazy bus driver planted a bomb. Maybe—"

Suddenly, Nancy and her friends found themselves alone as the rest of the tour dived for cover inside the restaurant as they took in Bess's words.

"Now look what you've done, Bess," George teased. "You'll have everybody climbing trees in a minute. Will you stop talking about bombs?"

"I can't help it if I'm allergic to things that blow up," Bess replied.

"Nothing's going to blow up." George sighed. "Except maybe my head. You've given me a terrible headache."

"What do you think, Nancy?" the professor cut in, as the onlookers continued to stare at the bus which was starting to rock slightly from whatever was causing the uproar inside.

A smile broke over the young detective's face. "No," she said, "I don't think it's a bomb or anything dangerous. Stay here a minute. I believe we can solve this mystery very simply."

Nancy ran to the bus, opened the front door and reached inside to grab a large key dangling from the steering column. Immediately, she hurried to the luggage doors and unlocked them. As they fell open, everyone gasped with relief and surprise.

Inside, tangled up with the baggage, was a man in

long red underwear. He was bound hand and foot with his own belt and tie, and judging from the color of his face and the muffled sounds coming through the gag in his mouth, he was furious.

"Some bomb," George said.

"Well, who is he?" Bess asked, beginning to calm down from her fright.

"I wager he's the real bus driver," George offered.

"You're right," Nancy said, as the man's gag was removed and, in a torrent of surprisingly good English, he let everyone within 500 yards know who he was. How dare they let a helpless man bounce around in a luggage compartment for almost two hours while a thief drove his bus! he exclaimed.

"But we didn't know," Bess protested. "Honestly. We heard a noise but—"

"You heard a noise! You heard a noise!" the indignant man repeated as he wrapped himself in a blanket provided by the restaurant owner. "Of course you heard a noise!"

"Well," Bess said, backing away defensively, "we told the driver and he said you were just a bunch of loose tools bouncing around. I mean, not that *you* were loose tools but that's what the noise was. Oh, I can't explain. Nancy, help me," the girl wailed.

"Loose tools!" screamed the little bus driver, now almost dancing with frustration. "You should have realized that he wasn't telling the truth," he added, grinding his teeth. "Did he look like a bus driver? No! Now *I* look like a bus driver."

As everyone gaped at him, his eyes traveled down his body, which was wrapped in the blanket with his bare feet sticking out. Again his face turned red, and he angrily shouted once more. "That's right, stare at me. Embarrass me. Get me my clothes!"

Ned moved in to assist. "I'll take him inside," he said, "and I'll see if the people here have some spare clothes to lend him. I'll be back." He put his arm consolingly around the man's shoulders. "Sir," he said, "you have been through a terrible ordeal. We are very sorry. Let me help you. Come with me and we'll get some clothes for you and some lunch."

"Don't touch the bus," the driver cried, waving a warning finger at the others as Ned led him away. "I will assume command again when I return."

When he and Ned finally disappeared into the restaurant, the whole group broke out laughing.

"Don't touch his bus!" George smirked.

Bess, completely recovered now, resumed her old, humorous ways. "Hey, George, didn't I tell you there was a *bomb* in that bus?"

Again the young people laughed.

"You were right," Eric said. "If that wasn't an explosion I don't know what to call it. But seriously, it must have been pretty frightening being tied up and gagged like that, worrying what was going to happen to you."

Bess, who was standing close to Nancy, whispered, "You see what I mean. He's really a very sensitive boy—and you know what?"

"What?" said Nancy.

"I think he's developing a crush on you."

"Oh, Bess, stop it." The young sleuth chuckled.

Their joking, however, was interrupted by Professor Bagley who said he wanted to talk to Nancy. They strolled together along a grassy path.

"I'm glad you remember that we never did finish our conversation," Nancy said. She smiled eagerly. "You left me hanging back there when Bess came running in shouting about the bus. The last thing you told me was that you wanted them to steal your luggage."

"Can you guess why?"

"Yep." Nancy grinned. "I think so."

"Okay." The professor laughed. "Let's hear it."

"Well," Nancy said, "my guess is that someplace in your luggage was something you wanted them to find, that would throw them off the track of the ten children."

"Bull's-eye," Dr. Bagley said softly. "Absolutely on target. What I did, purposely, of course, was to let them watch me slip a sealed envelope into my musette bag, that over-the-shoulder bag I've carried ever since army days. It's army issue, you know. Anyway, that envelope contains very authentic-looking documents which give all the wrong information about where the children are, how many there are, and most important of all, the wrong time and place at which they will cross the border."

"And they fell for it," Nancy said.

"Sure. I wasn't too obvious about planting it in the bag. What I did was to go in the men's room at Kennedy Airport in New York, carrying the envelope and my bag. When I came out, I only had the bag. I looked like a typical, clumsy amateur attempting to conceal something."

Nancy covered her eyes with both hands and pretended to wail. "Oh, I really did it, didn't I? You had them set up so nicely and then I and my friends came along and ruined the whole thing."

The professor shook his head. "No, no, no. They'll try again, so don't worry. I'll make the phony information available for them again—not too available, though. I'm willing to bet that within two days they will have found it. In fact, next time I'll give them time to read it, replace it, and make it look as if nothing had been touched."

Nancy nodded. "That's very clever, Professor. You must have been a good spy during the war."

He shook his head. "Actually, I was a very bad spy. People who are six feet six and need glasses can't exactly fade into the scenery. Sometimes I wonder how I came through it all without getting caught."

Strolling back to the hotel, they found the driver outfitted in a set of oversize clothing provided by the innkeeper. With a full stomach and lavish praise from everyone, the driver soon became very talkative and friendly.

As he headed the bus once again down the highway toward Salzburg, he entertained the group with a nonstop monologue about the beauties of the south German and Austrian countryside, the glorious musical traditions of the city of Salzburg, and most important, the life of the driver's personal hero, the great composer Wolfgang Amadeus Mozart.

"He was born in Salzburg, you know," the driver called out so that all could hear. "Born in that beautiful little city on January 27, 1756. He was a genius! A genius! I tell you!

"He played the harpsichord by the time he was four, composed music at the age of five, performed before the empress at the court in Vienna when he was six.

"He never went to school. Imagine that! *Never went to school*. His entire life was music. He performed as a child prodigy in concert tours throughout Europe.

"But as he grew older, the novelty wore off. Though he was composing the greatest music ever heard, no one seemed to care because by then, he was a grown-up."

The driver was now building himself up to a fever pitch similar to his mood when he was released from the luggage compartment. His knuckles gripped the wheel tightly, and he was starting to run off the road occasionally as he waved first one and then both hands in the air.

"He tried to seek his fortune in Vienna, got married and had children, but could not get a regular job. Will you believe that, young people? The most gifted composer the world has ever known—a superb performer as well—and the world ignored him. They ignored the man who composed *Don Giovanni!* The man who composed *The Magic Flute!* Forty symphonies. More than six hundred works in all!

"And they did not give him enough to support his family. He died in poverty at the age of thirty-five!"

The little man turned completely around and shouted the words, running off the road once more and causing an intake of breath by everyone on board.

"In poverty!" the driver bellowed, once he had the bus back on the road again.

"Oh, Nancy," George whispered. "In a way, I wish we had the other driver back. I wish he'd steal the bus."

"At the age of thirty-five!" the driver exclaimed.

"And they buried him in potter's field in a pauper's grave with no marker so that to this day," and he turned again to shout the words, "to this day no one knows where his body lies! The greatest composer of all time and one of the ten greatest men who ever lived! Wolfgang Amadeus Mozart! When you go to Salzburg to the cathedral, bow your heads and say a little prayer for the souls of those who denied him fame and fortune while he lived!"

Suddenly, the man lapsed into a brooding silence and said no more all the way to Salzburg. The passengers, who had been tense, braced for an accident, suddenly felt themselves go limp with relief.

Bess spoke first. "You know," she told Nancy, "he scared me to death and I wouldn't want to go through it again but I have to admire his passion for Mozart. I didn't know those things about him."

Nancy smiled. "Neither did I. I guess that's the first bit of education we're going to get on this tour."

"I suppose so," Bess said, "but I hope the rest of it moves at a slower pace."

Gradually, conversation picked up and the rest of the trip into Salzburg was spent talking, singing, and admiring the countryside. When they pulled into the ancient town, they headed immediately for their hotel and disembarked, somewhat tired but looking forward to baths and a good dinner.

As the driver and porters were unloading the luggage, the professor went inside to register the group. In five minutes he reappeared, clearly irritated.

"Attention! I have some unfortunate news. The hotel says that they received a call about four hours ago canceling our reservations. We have no rooms for tonight!"

4

Mysterious Interference

For a moment, the group stood stunned by the professor's announcement. Then everyone tried to talk at once.

"No rooms? How are we going to brush our teeth?"

"Or take a bath?"

"Or do my nails?"

"Or sleep?"

"Wait! Wait! Wait!" Dr. Bagley called. He held up his hands, quieting them down. "The hotel manager has assured me that he will make every attempt to see that we get proper accommodations at another hotel. He understands that we're the victims of practical jokers. Now if we will keep our

40

heads, we can muddle through. So let's go back inside and splash some water on our faces in the lobby rest rooms and freshen up a bit. We'll be able to have a lovely dinner while the hotel stores our baggage and makes other arrangements."

"Excuse me, Herr Professor." The speaker was a rather stout man with a huge, black mustache and an easy, smiling manner. "Excuse me. Professor Bagley? I couldn't help overhear your conversation with the desk clerk when you checked in. Permit me to introduce myself. I am Herr Adolph Gutterman. I think I may be able to help you."

Hesitantly, the professor extended his hand. "Pleased to meet you, I'm sure. But I think we're being taken care of quite adequately."

Herr Gutterman looked doleful. "Oh, Professor, excuse me, but I don't think that's true. Of course, the hotel will try. But this is the height of the tourist season. Every hotel is booked to overflowing!" He laughed and made a sweeping gesture. "The hotel will not be able to help you. But I can."

Dr. Bagley was obviously becoming annoyed by Herr Gutterman's insistent manner. "Well, perhaps so," he said, a little coolly, "but let's give the hotel a chance. Now, if you'll excuse me, my people are famished. We must go in to dinner."

Moving right in step with the professor, Herr Gutterman was not to be put off. "Excellent idea,"

41

he cried, thumping him on the back. "I'm hungry, too. I'll join you and explain how I can assist you."

Resigned to his fate, the professor forced a smile and nodded, being too well mannered to be rude even though Herr Gutterman was obviously proving himself a pest.

As they passed the desk, Herr Gutterman received a look of irritation from the manager. The fat man returned it with a wide smile and said, in a booming voice, "Yes, it's a shame that we have hotels in Salzburg that fail to honor their reservations, but there are always a few rotten apples in every barrel."

The manager, watching Herr Gutterman virtually take charge of Professor Bagley's group, snapped his pencil in anger.

Once in the dining room, Herr Gutterman proceeded to explain what he was offering without anyone having asked him to do so.

"I am in real estate," he announced, "and I deal in properties all over Austria. It so happens that I know a very nice, small hotel just a few blocks from here. I had reserved a large number of rooms, more than twenty, for another group that canceled out just this morning. I am offering you these rooms."

The offer was tempting, but the professor, completely put off by the loud, aggressive manner of the real estate man, refused to commit himself. "As I

42

said before," he repeated politely, "we'll wait to see what the hotel can do for us."

"Suit yourself, Herr Professor, suit yourself," boomed the realtor, again slapping the professor on the back.

George leaned over and whispered to Nancy, "I think if he whacks the professor once more there's going to be violence."

Nancy nodded. "You know, George, I think I've seen Herr Gutterman before, but I don't know where."

George looked at the realtor. "Hmm. If *I* had ever seen a two-hundred-fifty-pound, six-foot man with a big, black mustache and a loud voice like his, I think I'd remember where."

As they talked, Herr Gutterman kept up a running fire of conversation—or, rather, a monologue—as he told poor jokes, provided most of the laughter, then complained about the bad service and bragged about his vast wealth. By the time dinner was over, everyone was thoroughly sick of him.

To their astonishment, however, he picked up the check for the group and paid for it before anyone knew what he was doing. He then led the unwilling students out of the restaurant and back to the hotel manager's desk where he loudly banged on the bell despite the fact that the manager was standing less than three feet away.

"A little service, please," he rumbled.

"What is it, Herr Gutterman," the manager inquired icily.

"I wanted to know if you have obtained rooms for my friends on Professor Bagley's tour. If not, I shall escort these unfortunate people to my hotel and see that they are treated as all guests in Salzburg *should* be treated. I tell you, Herr Schoenburg, your hotel is a disgrace to the nation. A disgrace!"

"Weasel!" hissed the hotel manager. "How dare you come in here and behave this way. Bruckner! Bruckner!" A tall, strong young porter came striding across the room. "Escort Herr Gutterman out of the hotel."

Herr Gutterman, flashing his fat smile, held up both hands. "That won't be necessary. I am leaving. But you, my friends," he said, turning to Professor Bagley and his group, "can meet me on the sidewalk after this incompetent gives you his bad news."

With a flourish, Herr Gutterman waddled away through the doors and into the street. The manager, flushed with embarrassment, turned to the professor.

"Sir, I am chagrined to have to tell you that I cannot find you accommodations. Believe me, if I could do anything to make up for this terrible mistake, I would."

The professor nodded and rubbed his chin.

44

"What do you suggest we do? We must sleep. Tomorrow we begin our tour here in this city."

The manager passed one hand over his eyes. "Much as it pains me," he said, "I think you had better accept Herr Gutterman's offer."

Reluctantly, the professor agreed and the forlorn group filed out onto the sidewalk where Herr Gutterman, completely unperturbed by his recent dismissal from the hotel, was waiting with a smile and a bear hug for the professor.

"Now," he rumbled, "you come with me and you will be treated as honored guests." Subdued, the group followed Herr Gutterman down the street, instructing the bus driver to bring their bags as soon as possible.

To their surprise, the hotel, though small, was clean, neat, and pleasant in appearance. Nancy, Bess, and George were assigned a large room with bunk beds. Their bags arrived as they were testing the mattresses and checking whether the water faucets worked.

Leaving the other girls to unpack, Nancy went downstairs to make her long-delayed call to her father. But when she reached the phones in the lobby, she found they were in use and would be for some time since there was a long waiting line ahead of her.

The clerk on duty motioned her to come over to

the desk and told her that if she was in a hurry she could use the pay phone on the street half a block away. Nancy thanked him and hurried out the door, turning left and walking along the quiet, dimly lit street until she saw the booth. It was on the opposite side built against a high stone wall. Nancy entered, fumbled for her Austrian coins, and then dialed the number of her home in River Heights.

"Hello!" It was the cheerful, deep voice of her father, Carson Drew.

"Hi, Dad!"

"And who might this be?"

"Very funny. Who else calls you Dad?"

The lawyer laughed. "How are you, dear? How do you like Austria?"

"Beautiful. But so far our bus driver was kidnapped, a car almost ran over Ned, a man tried to steal the professor's luggage, and somebody canceled our hotel reservations."

Her father groaned. "Well, it sounds like a typical trip for my Nancy. Do you know why all these things have been happening?"

Nancy hesitated. Dr. Bagley had sworn her to secrecy about the orphans, and she couldn't violate her promise. "Well," she said, "let's say I'm working on it, Dad. But tell me about Vienna and the stolen film. It sounds fascinating."

Carson Drew proceeded to outline the case. Kurt Kessler, a noted film director from an Eastern Eu-

46

ropean country, had defected to America more than a year before. He had managed to smuggle out several valuable reels of film, which he had since edited into a documentary condemning the oppression of human rights in his native land. The film was entered in a very important film festival to be held in Vienna during the coming week.

"This morning," Carson Drew said, "Kessler received a call from the festival authorities. His film has been stolen. Unless he can recover it by Wednesday morning, the world will not see or hear his story."

"But why can't he get another print made from the negative and rush that to Vienna?" the girl detective asked.

"He thought of that, of course," her father said. "Unfortunately somebody on the other side thought of it, too. Kessler made the mistake of leaving his negative at a laboratory for printing. He should have stayed with it to protect it. But he didn't, and an hour later the laboratory burned to the ground. The negative was destroyed. The stolen film, if it still exists, is the only copy of Kurt Kessler's *Captive Witness*."

Nancy whistled. "But if government enemies stole it," she said, "don't you think they destroyed it right away or at least took it out of Austria? After all, that fire in the lab was probably a case of arson."

"Right," Mr. Drew said.

"So we're probably on a wild-goose chase," Nancy said, somewhat crestfallen.

"No, I don't think so. I have reason to believe that Kessler's enemies will take good care of the film because they want to trade it for something even more valuable to them."

"But what?"

"That," the lawyer said, "is what my beautiful, talented daughter is going to have to figure out."

"I appreciate the compliment, Dad, but what I need are some solid leads."

Carson Drew sighed. "Well, I wish I had some. The best I can offer is one contact. His name is Richard Ernst and he's the official at the film festival who can tell you the details about the theft. Contact him at the festival office. That's about all I can tell you. Oh, except for one thing. Be careful and watch out for two enemy operatives. One is tall, heavy-featured, with blond hair and blue eyes. The other is shorter, wiry. He has a bad complexion. Pitted skin."

Nancy almost dropped the phone. "Oh, Dad, say no more. I think I know the fun-loving pair personally."

"You do!"

"Yes. I wish I could explain on the phone but—" Nancy stopped. "Dad! Dad, did you hear that? It sounded as if someone were tapping this line."

There was a long pause and then her father's voice came through. "That's not possible on this end, Nancy. Remember we had our phone system constructed to make taps impossible? And at great expense, I might add." There was another pause. "Nancy, be careful. If there is a tap, it's on your end."

A chill ran up the girl's spine. She wondered how it could have been done so quickly. No one knew she was calling from a public phone booth. Then she remembered how the hotel clerk had specifically beckoned her to the desk and told her about the pay phone. It had been a setup!

"Dad," she said. "Dad?" There was no answer. She jiggled the hook. "Dad, can you hear me? Dad?" After a few seconds, she gave up and tried to dial again but the line was completely dead now.

As she hung up, something banged and scraped violently across the top of the phone booth and the light went out. Suddenly, Nancy found herself alone on the almost completely darkened street as the figure of a tall man moved slowly, purposefully, toward her.

5

An Unpleasant Invitation

"Nancy Drew! What are you doing standing in a dark phone booth at this hour of the night?" The threatening, tall figure peered into the booth, and much to Nancy's relief, she realized it was Dr. Bagley.

"That's a good question." The young sleuth sighed. "I was talking to my dad back in River Heights. Then I thought I heard a tap on the line. But he reminded me that our house has special equipment to prevent tapping at his end, so it must've been on mine.

"But look." She pointed up at the line running from the booth. "I don't see any taps. And anyway, right after that, the line went dead, the light switched off, and I heard a crash on top of the booth."

The professor peered up. "It was just the branch scraping across that broke the light wire. I don't see any phone lines so they're probably all underground, which rules out a wiretap. I think you're just a little edgy about everything that's happened."

Nancy bit her lip, concentrating hard. "You're right," she acknowledged, "but what were you doing walking out here alone?"

"I was going to use the telephone."

"Why didn't you use one in the hotel?"

"Well, there were too many people waiting."

"And did the desk clerk call you over and tell you to use the pay phone down the street?"

"Yes. Did he tell you, too?"

"Uh-huh. Isn't that odd?"

The professor thought for a moment. "Yes, it is. But not as odd as the question of why they would tap a pay phone when they could so easily tap the phone in the hotel."

"You've got me. I'm dizzy thinking about it, Professor. Let's say it was all my imagination and we can both go to bed early and get some sleep."

The professor escorted Nancy back to the hotel. When she opened the door to her room, she found Bess and George both sound asleep. Very quietly, so as not to wake them, she got out her pajamas and toilet articles and prepared for bed. But when she lay down, she couldn't go to sleep right away. The tangled events of the day kept marching through her mind. She hadn't bothered to unpack because she knew that first thing in the morning she had to make plans to leave the tour and drive to Vienna. Then she could try to locate Kurt Kessler's missing film before the Wednesday deadline.

On the other hand, she thought, I feel bad about leaving Dr. Bagley when the tour is being harassed and he still hasn't figured out how to get those poor kids across the border.

Tossing and turning, the girl detective finally drifted off to sleep, exhausted by the events of the day.

The next morning, she was awakened by Bess's exuberant bubbling about Salzburg. "Nancy, are you still asleep? Listen, I don't want to miss anything! The cathedral. The puppet shows. The palace. The concerts. And Mozart's home. Oh, I couldn't miss *that!*"

"I agree," Nancy moaned sleepily. "If you did, our little bus driver would probably drive us all the way to Vienna screaming out another lecture about his hero."

"Right," Bess agreed. "Now, when are you two getting up? It's eight o'clock already."

"Eight o'clock?" came an agonized cry from under a pillow hiding George's head. "In the morning?

Oh, no! Nancy, do something. Stop her. She's killing us."

But Nancy, struggling to a sitting position, yawned and shook her head. "You can stay in bed, George, but I've got to get up."

"Great," Bess said. "Where do you want to go first, Nancy?"

"Vienna."

"Vienna?" the cousins chorused as George emerged out of the covers. "What do you mean Vienna?" she asked. "We're not due there until— when?"

"Sunday," Bess put in.

"And this is only Friday," George said.

"I know, I know," their friend said, heading for the bathroom. "Do you mind if I take my shower first? I really have to rush."

"Oh, no, you don't." Bess laughed, barring the bathroom door. "Not until you tell us about this Vienna stuff."

"Nancy Drew," George said slowly, pointing a forefinger at the young detective, "are you going off to solve another mystery and leave us alone on this tour?"

"Well . . ." Nancy said.

"That's it," George said. "I knew it. And I suppose you can't talk about it."

"Only a little bit. Somebody stole a film from the festival that opens in Vienna Wednesday and I'm trying to find it. There. No secrets. Okay?"

"Humph," Bess said. "And all those huddles—you and the professor and—and handsome, young Eric. What were they all about?"

Nancy raised her nose in the air, pretending total bewilderment. "I'm sure I don't know what you may be referring to," she said with a theatrical swirl of her robe, and disappeared into the bathroom to the echoes of her friends' laughter.

After breakfast, Nancy began phoning car rental agencies and to her chagrin, found that there wasn't a single car available.

She came back and joined her friends in the restaurant. "No luck," she said. "This is really awful. I don't know how I'm going to get to Vienna unless I take a bus."

"Would that be so terrible?" George asked.

"No. It's just that when I arrive in Vienna I'll probably need a car to get around."

"You could not get on a bus," came a booming voice they all recognized. It was Herr Gutterman struggling up out of the depths of an armchair that had concealed even his massive bulk. He waddled over to their table and, making an elaborate, somewhat comic bow, he said good morning.

"May I sit down with you lovely ladies?" he asked, and then pulled out a chair before anyone could reply. "Ah, I thank you. Now, Miss Drew, you must not think of taking a bus to Vienna. You

54

have no idea how crowded they are at this time. Probably you would have to stand, and who wants to stand when they are on their vacation, *ja?*"

Nancy smiled sweetly. "I don't think I have much choice."

"Ah, but you do, beautiful lady! I myself will see that you get to Vienna in the perfect safety and comfort of my own automobile driven by my own chauffeur."

At this point, Ned Nickerson strode into the dining room. The sound of the boorish Herr Gutterman offering Nancy a ride to Vienna made him almost trip and spill the cup of coffee he was carrying.

Continuing to smile sweetly at Herr Gutterman and looking over his shoulder directly at Ned, Nancy said, "Herr Gutterman, that is extremely nice of you. I accept your offer if we can leave within the next hour or two."

Both Bess and George had to struggle hard not to say something, and Nancy felt George's foot nudge her own under the table.

"Excellent, excellent," Herr Gutterman bellowed as he heaved himself to his feet. "I will make arrangements immediately and we shall leave—at noon?"

"That would be wonderful," Nancy said. "Thank you so very much."

Rubbing his hands with pleasure, Herr Gutterman left the hotel while Ned rushed over and sank down in the vacated seat.

"Nancy," he said, his eyes filled with disbelief, "*you* are going to accept a ride to Vienna with *that man?*"

"Yes," Nancy replied, her eyes twinkling. "What's so upsetting about that?"

Ned began to feel hot under the collar. "You and that two-ton creep?" he asked again, his voice rising. "Wait a minute. Let's back up. Why *are* you going to Vienna today? Another detective assignment?"

Nancy nodded.

"In the middle of our tour? Oh, now, Nancy." Then he remembered his original objection. "And you're going with Gutterman?"

Nancy couldn't contain her laughter any longer and she doubled up.

"What's so funny?" Ned cried, genuinely upset.

"Nothing, nothing." She giggled. "And don't get all strung out. Here's the joke on Herr Gutterman. I want *you* to go with me to Vienna! Just imagine Gutterman's face when he sees both you and me waiting for him! You will come, won't you?"

6

Kidnapped!

Ned's face changed from a look of intense anxiety to one of such unrestrained happiness that all three girls began laughing.

"Very funny, Nancy Drew," said Ned. "Very funny. You are the worst tease I ever met. Now what would you do if I said no?"

Nancy wrinkled her nose at him. "I suppose I'd have to drop into a hole in the earth when Herr Gutterman came to pick me up. You wouldn't let that happen, would you?"

"Of course he wouldn't," George said. "He would follow you to the ends of the earth."

"To Vienna, anyway," Ned declared.

The young people split up, Nancy and Ned making their good-byes and explaining to Professor Bagley that they would meet him and the tour in Vienna on Sunday. At noon, they were both standing in front of the hotel with their bags.

Within a few minutes, a beautiful brown sedan pulled up with Herr Gutterman at the wheel. He was beaming happily as he fought his way out from under the steering wheel which pressed against his bulging stomach.

Hurrying around the car, he picked up Nancy's bags and placed them in the trunk. As he did so, Nancy glanced around for Ned. He was gone! And Herr Gutterman was opening the rear door and gesturing for her to enter and be seated.

"Oh," Nancy said, "could you wait a moment, please? I've forgotten something." Turning, she dashed back into the hotel where Bess and George were watching the scene through a window.

"Did you lose something, Nancy?" Bess giggled.

"Where is Ned?" Nancy cried.

"Oh, Ned!" Bess said. "You're looking for Ned?"

"Come on, you two, what are you doing to me?" She stopped. "Oh, I get it. He's getting even for my teasing this morning. Okay, I apologize. Now please tell me where he is."

Ned appeared, almost magically, at Nancy's elbow. "Oh, Nancy, I'm so sorry." He grinned. "I just wanted to make sure you really wanted me to go."

"Oh, you!" Nancy laughed.

The two young people hurried outside where Herr Gutterman waited impatiently. Nancy smiled at him. "Herr Gutterman, I hope you won't mind, but my friend Ned Nickerson also has to go to Vienna. I thought that with so much room in your big car perhaps you wouldn't mind giving him a lift, too."

"I'd very much appreciate it," Ned said, using his most humble tone.

The barest flicker of annoyance passed over Herr Gutterman's face, but he quickly covered it by laughing loudly, assuring Ned he was delighted. For good measure, he slapped him on the back—a bit harder than necessary.

With great ceremony, he ushered them into the back seat, then trotted around front and squeezed himself into the driver's seat. He called through the speaking tube into the rear seat. "You will pardon me if I do the driving myself until we pick up my chauffeur. He is on the other side of town."

"Perfectly all right," Nancy called, settling back in the plush interior. "What a beautiful car," she said. "I see that it's been freshly painted." Some of the paint had come off on Nancy's finger as she touched the door.

"Yes," Herr Gutterman replied, "I try to keep my cars looking new."

"Hmm," Ned said, "a refrigerator, a telephone, a television set. Herr Gutterman, you travel in style."

Nancy noted a clicking sound. Herr Gutterman

had locked all the doors electronically. Well, thought Nancy, nothing unusual about that. Dad's car operates that way. Even so, the gesture made her uneasy.

As they crossed Salzburg and slowed down to enter an alley adjoining an old building, a warning sounded in her brain. A freshly painted car. Why? A ride to Vienna. Why? Hotel rooms just when they needed them. Why was this seemingly innocuous pest so solicitous of the Americans?

Nancy felt a shiver as Ned said, "Nancy, do you hear the engine of this car?"

"No."

They both realized, simultaneously, what this meant. "Like the black car," Ned whispered. "The same silent engine."

"It's the same car, Ned. They painted it yesterday. The paint is still wet—and the doors are locked."

Who was this Gutterman?

As Nancy asked the question, the car pulled up to a doorway and a man dashed out. Gutterman squeezed out from behind the driver's seat and the chauffeur slid in, turning to stare at Nancy and Ned. They gasped as they realized he was the short, wiry man with the pitted face—the man who had stolen the bus in Munich.

Now the fat man began to take off his coat. Underneath he wore great pads that, as he slipped them off, made him lose seventy-five pounds in appearance. Next he removed his wig and began tugging at his mustache. With blond hair, no mustache, and considerably lighter in weight, he was the same man who had attempted the luggage theft at the Munich airport.

"I can't believe it," Ned murmured.

"Well, we saw it with our own eyes," Nancy said. "And I thought I was so clever to get Herr Gutterman to drive us to Vienna."

"Yeah," Ned said. "Now what?"

"Relax, I guess," the girl detective said, "while we try to figure a way out."

"But there is nothing you can do, Nancy Drew," came Gutterman's voice through the communications system. "The doors are locked. The windows are tinted so that you can see out but no one can see into the rear compartment. I can see you by switching on a secret electrical impulse which clears the window separating us. All I have to do is press the button."

"Don't worry, Nancy," Ned whispered, "we've got to stop sometime, and there are bound to be cars nearby. Then we'll yell our heads off. Someone will notice us."

Nancy nodded and then, as luck would have it, they found themselves side by side with a police car at a red light. Instantly, the two young people set up the loudest racket they could.

"Help us!" Ned cried. "Help! Help!"

"We're being kidnapped," Nancy yelled.

But the more they shouted the less effect it seemed to have. The policemen sat, talking casually to each other. Not once did they turn in the right direction. At last, the police car drove away and Herr Gutterman's annoying voice broke in on them again.

"You shouldn't shout like that." Gutterman laughed. "You'll ruin your voices. It's futile, because the rear compartment is completely sound-proofed. I guess I forgot to tell you that. In fact, it is airtight. If air were not pumped in to you constantly, you could not breathe."

"What do you intend to do with us, Herr Gutterman—or whatever your name is?" Nancy questioned, looking at him, her blue eyes now like ice.

"Herr Gutterman is as good a name as any," their captor said. "My chauffeur is Herr Burger. As to what we will do with you, well, we will take you to a place where you will not be able to meddle in matters that don't concern you. Whether you ever come back, I have not yet decided."

7

Hazardous Ride

Resigned to the fact that they could do nothing until their captors, at some point, opened the doors, Nancy and Ned did their best to relax as the silent brown car headed south and began climbing higher and higher into the magnificent Austrian Alps.

Since every word could be monitored by Herr Gutterman, the couple talked of trivial matters while at the same time writing surreptitious notes on the pad Nancy kept in her bag.

"Lovely weather, isn't it?" Nancy asked as she scrawled a note.

"Charming," Ned replied as he watched Nancy's words form on the page. "Charming. And with such delightful traveling companions."

Ned, Nancy had written, *they must stop eventually if only to stretch their legs. When they do, let's remember that I have this.* Nancy pointed to a small, innocent-looking book with a blue cover which she held in her lap. She turned it slightly and Ned saw that along the spine, in the middle of the title, there were actually small holes cut out of the center of two *o*'s. The title made Ned grin: *Noodles.*

Ned took the pad from Nancy, very casually, and scribbled his reply. *Haven't read the book. But I loved the movie. Why the holes?*

Nancy took back the pad and wrote two words: *Tear gas.* Reading them, Ned could hardly restrain himself. He wanted to shout but refrained. Instead, he wrote on the pad, *Cleverest girl in River Heights. When the time comes, try to spray the big guy. I'll jump the little fellow.*

My hero, Nancy wrote, stifling a giggle. *Why don't you jump the big one?*

"Beautiful scenery," Ned said aloud. "Do you suppose Herr Gutterman and Herr Burger appreciate it?"

"Why, of course," Nancy said, adding, "I bet that before this trip is over, you'll find tears in their eyes."

Herr Gutterman, who could hear everything they said, guffawed. "Enjoy the view, little ones," he called out. "Enjoy it while you can."

"Is that a threat?" Nancy asked coolly.

"Oh, let's say, a final warning," Gutterman rasped.

"A warning about what?" Nancy asked, baiting the man. "What were we doing that could ever justify our abduction?"

"Abduction? Oh, my, my, my, what a harsh word."

"That's what the police would call it," Ned chimed in.

"The police! The police are so stupid and slow. You and I, Nancy Drew, are much quicker than the police. Much brighter."

"Very flattering," Nancy said, "but I know too many policemen who catch too many people like you, so I can't buy that line."

Gutterman laughed. "Like the ones in the police car a little while ago?" He roared again. "We don't worry about the police, but we do worry about people who have big ideas."

"Big ideas about what?" Nancy persisted, trying to find out just how much Gutterman knew of her activities. What, if anything, did he know about the mission to save the orphans; and did he also know about Nancy's personal mission to find the stolen documentary, *Captive Witness*? Or was it possible that he was involved in some unknown project that concerned neither the orphans nor the film?

Whatever the answers, Herr Gutterman remained silent, refusing to be drawn out on the subject. He sat sideways, keeping his eyes riveted on them, his mouth twisted in a mysterious, sardonic grin.

As the car climbed higher, the road became more dangerous. They began traveling along two lines cut out of the mountainside with sheer cliffs falling away into beautiful, lush, green valleys across which wandered lovely, clear streams fed by the melting glaciers and snows of the Austrian Alps.

Traffic was sparse with no cars traveling in their direction and only an occasional car or truck coming the other way. The open road made Herr Burger feel slightly exhilarated.

"I'm a bit bored with this slow driving," he called back to them. "I think I'll show you how experienced Alpine drivers take these roads."

"Here we go." Ned groaned. "A Saturday night cowboy. They've got them all over the world, I guess."

"Just hang on," Nancy said. "No matter what Herr Burger does, I'm sure he wants to stay alive just as much as we do."

Within the next few minutes, the couple began to doubt whether that was true. Herr Burger speeded up until he had the beautiful car careening around turns, spraying dust, pebbles, and bits of tire rubber into the air. Then, roaring down a relatively straight stretch of road, he threw the car into a skidding loop that took them within six inches of a cliff edge where there was no guardrail. Herr Gutterman's only response was a bemused look and a question thrown over his shoulder at his captives.

"Do you enjoy this, Miss Drew? Your friend seems a little blue around the lips."

"Sorry about that," Ned said. "I always turn blue when I'm happy."

"Is this fast enough for you, Miss Drew, or would you like Herr Burger to speed up? Are you frightened, Miss Drew? We wouldn't want to frighten you."

Nancy looked at Ned. "He's unbelievable," she said. "He's like some childish villain out of a bad movie."

"Miss Drew? You're not frightened, are you?" The noise of the squealing brakes and the flying gravel were making it difficult for Gutterman to hear them up front where the windows were open. He was gazing back at her, smiling cruelly.

"No, no, I'm not frightened," Nancy said, swinging wildly and hanging on to the strap. "Mr. Nickerson and I are terribly impressed, as a matter of fact."

Gutterman's face flushed beet-red. "Oh, is that so?" he snarled. "We'll see how impressed you are when we start questioning you."

"Oh, please don't question us," Ned cried mockingly.

Gutterman grew extremely angry at his prisoners'

refusal to show fear. His anger finally intensified to the breaking point when Herr Burger, negotiating another dangerous, screaming turn, caused Herr Gutterman to bang his head sharply against the window.

The big man let fly a stream of German invective mixed with French and German phrases that gave Nancy the impression that Gutterman was calling Burger a lunatic and moron. Burger was so upset, he wound up swerving into the opposite lane where the car faced a huge truck coming the other way.

For a split second, it appeared the two vehicles would collide but at the last moment both drivers veered sharply and barely missed each other. The danger of a head-on smash, however, was avoided at the price of a worse possibility. Herr Burger, completely rattled, was now driving straight toward the edge of a cliff!

"Look out!" Nancy and Ned cried with one voice as they both dropped down to the floor and covered their heads to minimize injuries in an accident.

As they crouched there, doubled over, they felt the car veer violently again, and heard a splintering, crunching sound. The car stopped, and there was silence.

Nancy was the first to bring her head slowly up to look out the window. "Oh, Ned," she gasped quietly, "We'd better start praying. Look where we are."

8

Danger in the Alps

"Don't move!" It was Gutterman's voice, trembling and filled with fear. "Don't even breathe."

All four passengers had good reason to obey the order because the car had gone partially through the guardrail and was teetering over the cliff. It's right rear wheel hung out in space and the left one was poised on the very edge.

"Let's get out of here," Burger cried, starting to climb out on his side, which was safely on the road.

Gutterman stopped him with a snarl. "If you lay one foot on the ground, I'll make you wish you were never born!"

"But what can we do?" Burger whined.

Gutterman pondered the question carefully. "It

seems to me that you and I can't get out because the weight of our friends in back will then topple the car right over the edge."

"You could open the back door on your side, Herr Burger. Just push the switch and unlock it, and Ned and I will get out slowly. Then you can get out, too," Nancy said steadily.

"No, you don't," Gutterman responded. "You two might make it and Burger could jump. With all the motion, the car would go over and take me with it."

"Well, you can't get out your side," Nancy pointed out. "You'd step into space, just as I would."

"No," Gutterman decided. "This is what we will do. Both of you should move as far over to the left as you can. I will climb over Burger and stand on the running board. Then, Burger, you start it up and see if the four-wheel drive can pull us out of this."

"Wait a minute," Ned protested. "If that doesn't work, you and Burger can jump free, but Nancy and I will go over the edge with the car."

"How clever you are," Gutterman sneered. "You do catch on quickly. That should make you both want to hug the left side of the car with all your might."

With no other choice, Nancy and Ned flattened themselves against the left side. The car tilted and rocked slightly.

71

"The worst is yet to come," Nancy breathed through her almost clenched teeth, "when that big galumph Gutterman tries to crawl over Burger. If he makes one slip, we'll really rock!"

"Don't think about it," Ned said. "Just squeeze yourself against this door."

Holding their breath, they froze as Gutterman, with surprising grace, managed to climb over Burger and out onto the left running board of the car. He hung off as far as he could, bearing his weight down fully, then told Burger to put the car in gear.

Burger did as he was ordered. Slowly, almost imperceptibly, the big, brown car began to move, its left rear wheel sending some gravel and rocks into the valley as it slipped slightly. The whole car tilted and, with a soft lunge, pulled up until the right rear wheel spun into contact with the ground and rolled to safety.

"Masterful driving," Gutterman said, patting his henchman on the shoulder. From the back seat, neither Ned nor Nancy let up on their tormentors.

"Oh, masterful," Nancy said. "Wasn't it, Ned?"

"Wonderful. Almost as good as the way he was driving when he went through the guardrail."

The two young people strived to make their captors so angry that they would open the back door to get at them. Nancy's plan could then be activated. While Ned attacked, she would fire her tear-gas "book" and perhaps they could finally escape.

But Gutterman and Burger were in a self-congratulatory mood. They even began singing as Burger continued to take the car higher into the mountains, this time at a more reasonable speed.

After several hours of driving, however, Burger pulled the car off on a dirt road and drove to what appeared to be a shepherd's hut. He stopped about a hundred feet away and turned around, almost backing over an extremely steep gorge in the process.

Nancy gulped again. "I don't know what they're going to do to us, Ned, but whatever it is, it has to be better than being locked in a high-powered automobile driven by Herr Burger."

"Absolutely," Ned concurred. "But what do you suppose they have in mind?"

The young couple soon found out as both Burger and Gutterman got out and walked around to the right-hand back door. "Now," Gutterman rasped as he unlocked the door with one hand while keeping the other thrust threatingly in his coat pocket, "you get out, Miss Drew. And you, Mr. Nickerson, you stay far over on the other side of the car if you know what's good for you."

Ned glanced down at Gutterman's pocket. Was there a gun inside? he wondered. Reading Ned's mind, the girl detective cautioned him.

"Don't do anything, Ned, please."

"Where are you taking her?" the young man demanded.

Gutterman flashed his evil smile, but said nothing. When Nancy got out, the door was shut and locked. Ned was left alone, helplessly watching the two men lead Nancy toward the shack.

But as she entered what appeared to be a crude building, she was amazed to find it beautifully cozy with sparkling, waxed floors, a cheery fireplace, a pretty rug, and upholstered furniture.

"Being a shepherd must pay very well," Nancy murmured, gesturing at the expensive furnishings. "But the shepherd doesn't own this anymore, does he?" she added, looking hard at Gutterman. "The wolves have taken over."

Gutterman shrugged. "Wolves. Sheep. I have no time for your small talk, Miss Drew. Let's get down to business."

"Excuse me," Nancy said, "but it was a long drive up here. Do you have a powder room where I could freshen up a bit?"

Gutterman pointed to a door at the far end of the room and, with an expansive bow, indicated that Nancy would find what she wanted there.

Will there be a window? she wondered. If so, will it be big enough for me to squeeze through? Her experienced eyes roved over every inch of the cottage searching for something, anything, that might produce a way out of the trap.

Once inside the bathroom, she saw there was no lock on the door. Obviously, Herr Gutterman had used this building for previous interrogations and didn't want his prisoners to lock themselves in while they plotted their next move.

Glancing swiftly around, she discovered a window but, unfortunately, it was high up and much too small even for a willowy eighteen-year-old.

After splashing water on her face, she dried off with a towel and looked in the mirror.

"Think, Nancy," she hissed. "Think. Don't just stand there."

Back outside in the living room, she found Herr Burger busily making coffee while Herr Gutterman lounged in a chair near the door. Apparently, Ned was still left behind in the car. Nancy noted quickly that the three windows in the room were all barred on the inside. Escape that way was impossible. Then she brightened. If escape through the window was impossible, then pursuit would be impossible, too. If only she could slip outside and lock the door behind her! Gutterman and Burger would be trapped!

Herr Gutterman was talking, babbling really, about his cleverness, and Nancy only half listened as she concentrated on escape.

The door to the room was made of solid oak, but Nancy had noticed a peculiar feature. On the outside walls were two metal slots like those found on cattle cars. They were used to hold a two-by-four or other heavy piece of timber across the door. Normally, such a crude but effective lock would be put inside a door to prevent forced entry. But obviously Herr Gutterman found himself constantly in need of locking people in, not keeping them out. Hence, the door to the building opened outward and could be blocked easily by dropping a piece of timber in the slots.

Instantly, Nancy flicked her eyes about the room looking for the timber to do the job. She saw it leaning against the doorjamb.

All she had to do was rise from her chair, pass Gutterman, grab the timber, open the door, slam it, and then throw the timber into place across the door.

She groaned inwardly. I'll never make it, she thought. But then Herr Gutterman said something that made her sit up straight.

"Of course," the man purred, "it would be advisable for you to answer my questions very quickly and correctly. You see, we left the engine of the car turned off. Therefore, no air will be fed into the back seat. Poor Mr. Nickerson. Who can say how long he will last?"

9

The Alpine Prison

Nancy quickly recovered and concealed her fright from Gutterman by flattering him. "Herr Gutterman," she said, "I don't know what line of business you are in, but I know you are much too cultured and urbane a gentleman to let an innocent person be injured. Why can't Ned be brought in here? You could tie him up. You don't have to hurt him."

Gutterman smiled. "You are a very clever girl, Nancy Drew. You know how to get your way. But this time, things will go better for you if we talk first. Besides, I'm sure Mr. Nickerson can last at least fifteen minutes. Now then, why are you mixed up in this ridiculous attempt to kidnap ten little children from Eastern Europe?"

"I don't know what you're talking about, Herr Gutterman; I'm not mixed up in anything."

"Your whole tour group is under suspicion," Gutterman continued. "Every one of you. But you most of all, because it would make sense for them to hire you for this job. If worse comes to worst, the charming Nancy Drew might charm the children across the border and charm the guards and charm everyone else."

Nancy continued to look calm but inside she was broiling. By the time this long-winded man finished asking three or four questions, Ned would be in real trouble, unable to breathe.

Her eyes, which had been trained on Gutterman's, now followed his hand down as he stubbed out his newly lit cigarette. It was then that she saw the car keys, lying on the table within easy reach. Fearing she would lose her courage if she hesitated, she took a deep breath and went into action.

Herr Burger had just put some iced coffee on the table in front of her and had gone back into the kitchen. With one swoop, Nancy grabbed the keys, flung her iced coffee into Herr Gutterman's face, and made a run for the door.

Gutterman was already on his feet and in pursuit. But then fate intervened as Herr Burger, hearing the glass shatter, rushed into the room, straight into the arms of Herr Gutterman. As they teetered, grunted, and crashed to the floor together, Nancy grabbed the timber and raced out the door. She had just enough time to slip the bar into place before she heard Gutterman smash against the solid oak, screaming.

To her relief, Ned was not only alive but yelling, trying to indicate that it was getting stuffy in his airless compartment.

She slammed the door and turned on the intercom. "Hang on, Ned, I'm looking for the ignition switch," she said.

Nancy began running her finger rapidly over the whole confusing array of switches and buttons. Finally, she found the starter, inserted the key, and pumped the accelerator. Nothing happened.

"Maybe it's flooded," Ned suggested.

"Oh," Nancy said in exasperation, "why does everyone always say that when you can't start a car?"

"Because that's generally what's wrong."

From the hut, Nancy could now hear noises which sounded like wild beasts fighting to claw and push their way out of captivity.

She laughed in spite of herself. "Apparently they don't like being locked up."

"I'll say," Ned shouted. "Look at that." As they watched the sturdy oak door, they saw a fist suddenly push right through it, shattering a plank completely. "Did you see that?" Ned asked. "And he's just warming up! Nancy, let's get out of here!"

"I'm trying." Again, the girl detective pressed on

the gas pedal and turned the key. Then a thought struck her. Some custom cars had a double ignition. One would have to be unlocked before the other one could work.

"Uh-oh," Ned said. "Look who's coming."

Nancy glanced up to see the enraged face of Herr Gutterman and the narrow, ratlike face of Herr Burger peering through the shattered door as Gutterman reached out to remove the timber blocking their exit.

"Nancy, what are we going to do? Listen, let me out!"

"That would be crazy!" Nancy cried. "No, I'll lock all the windows and doors. Then, at least, they can't get in."

The girl detective managed to hit the lock switches just in time.

Gutterman promptly threw a tantrum, pounding his fists, and finally his head, on the side of the car.

"You might as well give up," Nancy called. "You can't get in. Eventually, I'll get this started and when I do, it'll be bye-bye, Herr Gutterman."

Suddenly, Gutterman looked up. His hair was in disarray. His eyes were wild and red-rimmed. His tie was hanging down and his shirt was disheveled. But he let fly a cry of triumph.

"Aha," he shouted. "I'm not beaten yet." He darted in front of the car and lay down directly in its path. "Now try to get away!" he exclaimed. "You'll kill me, if you do, and you're too much of a lady to do that, aren't you, Miss Drew? Yes, I know you are. Your moral code wouldn't allow you to do something that might result in death or even bodily injury to another person, even to save your own life.

"That is why my kind wins and your kind loses these little battles, Miss Drew." Gutterman continued his lecture as his partner stared at him, unbelieving.

"Have you lost your mind?" Burger cried. "You *will* be killed, you maniac."

Nancy heard Gutterman, though neither she nor Ned could see him. "Not crazy," he bellowed. "You'll see."

But Herr Gutterman didn't know about the girl detective's superb driving skills and quick reflexes. While Gutterman was raving, Nancy found the second ignition. It was hidden behind a false cigarette lighter. She turned it quickly and then, quietly, slipped the key into the ignition itself.

"Ned," she whispered. "I've got it. Hold on, I'm going to start the car and back up like a rocket, then swing to the right."

"Got it," Ned replied softly. "Let's do it! I need air!"

In one swift and easy motion, Nancy started the engine, slammed the car into reverse, and went spinning back a dozen feet as soft pine needles slipped and churned under the wheels. Suddenly, the car slid downward as if on ice.

"It's the pine needles!" Ned shouted. "Quick, put it into first gear and the four-wheel drive will pull us out."

Smoothly, Nancy reversed the gears. The car shot forward and made a wide circle to the right, leaving the stricken Gutterman and Burger wailing in loud, shrill voices.

Out on the highway, Nancy pressed the big car to just under the speed limit and headed back for Vienna. From the back seat, she could hear Ned's voice. "Oh, that was tremendous! Tremendous! Let's go back and do it again, now that I can breathe. I want to see the looks on their faces."

"Once was enough." Nancy laughed as she pulled to the side of the road, unlocked the door switches, and made room for Ned in the front seat.

"Boy," Ned said, settling down, "it feels good to be out of the old cell, doesn't it? Well, anyway, now our worries are over."

"I don't know about that," Nancy said.

"Sure they are," Ned insisted. "We've got a nice car, we're headed for Vienna, we know that the people who are threatening the professor and the tour are really a bunch of muscleheads. They're not too smart, even if they do have beautiful cars and instant hotel reservations.

"By the way, why are they threatening the professor, and why are you going to Vienna? Do you realize I'm just stringing along with you, good old faithful Ned, and I don't even know what I'm getting myself into?"

"And I owe it to you to tell you," Nancy replied. As briefly as possible, she filled him in on the details of both the rescue effort involving the ten children and the mystery of the stolen film.

"Well, you'll figure everything out, Nancy. You always do. I have faith in you. If you need any heavy muscle work done, just call on your obedient slave."

"Thanks," Nancy said. "But right now, we're in trouble."

"What kind of trouble?"

"Well, just for starters, how about car theft?"

"Car theft? Those guys kidnapped us."

"Sure. But do we have any witnesses? Gutterman and Burger can claim they were nice enough to give us a ride and we took their car."

"But why would they want to draw attention to themselves?"

Nancy pondered the idea. "I suppose you're right, but even so, I don't want to be found with this car. I think we'll have to run the risk of leaving it someplace inconvenient."

"Gee, I hate to give up this beautiful buggy. Why don't we take our chances and explain it to the police if we have to? We'd be telling the truth."

Nancy shook her head. "We can't take any chances on this mission," she replied. "So this is where we get off."

"In the middle of nowhere? In the Austrian Alps?"

"Trust me," Nancy said.

10

Amphibian on Wheels

Nancy slowed down the big, brown car and at a small, almost hidden side road she pulled off. In a few moments, the car was lost from sight in the forest.

"Do you have any idea where we're going?" Ned asked.

"Not really," Nancy said, "but as we know, this car has four-wheel drive. It's obviously waterproof as well as soundproof and it's built high, providing a lot of space between the bottom of the car and the roadbed. That means we can drive it almost anywhere."

"Maybe even across a lake!" Ned chuckled.

"Don't laugh," Nancy said. "It could be amphibious and able to travel on water just like a boat!"

"In that case, did you pack an extra snorkel for me?" Ned teased.

"Not only that," Nancy said with a giggle, "but a set of flippers too!"

"Uh-oh, I'm beginning to think you're serious," Ned continued.

"I wish I were."

"Then I suggest we try hunting for another good road to Vienna," Ned said, "before we wind up in the drink!"

"Don't tell me you don't trust me, Ned," the young detective replied, eliciting no response from the boy.

They drove for almost an hour over the side road, which was little more than a pair of dusty ruts. It ended in a small stream about two feet wide.

"Now what?" Ned asked.

"We follow the stream," Nancy said. "Why?"

"Because streams always lead to people and houses, and anyone who gets lost in the woods should remember that." Ned laughed. "Oh, remember how they used to drill that into you at summer camp?"

"Yes," Nancy said, "and it happens to be absolutely true."

As the car bucked and lunged along the now grassy, now muddy streambed, Ned brought up the possibility of discovering a river large enough to float down. He had no sooner said it when they heard a rush of water and saw the little brook feed into a much larger stream, almost forty feet across.

"Well," said Ned, "here's where we find out whether we're riding in an amphibian."

"See those knobs and instructions?" Nancy asked. "This activates air pontoon sacks on the side, and this converts the engine power into a propeller drive shaft, which drops down when you push this button."

To their amazement, it all worked and they found themselves sailing grandly through the Austrian Alps in Herr Gutterman's beautiful automobile-boat. The thought made Nancy almost wistful.

"Ah, dear Herr Gutterman. What a trick we've played on him."

"It can't be helped," Ned said. "He really has to learn that he kidnapped the wrong people. He really—!"

"Shhh! Ned!"

The boy listened and gulped. "Is that sound what I think it is?"

Nancy nodded as the noise of raging water grew louder. "And I hope it isn't one of those two-hundred-foot Alpine monsters."

"Did you have to say that?" Ned asked worriedly. Suddenly, they tipped over the edge of a short fall that exploded into fast-moving rapids, which twist-

ed and turned the car so quickly that Nancy had all she could do to keep the nose pointed downstream.

"Is it leaking?" she yelled.

"I don't think so," Ned shouted. "Just some spray coming in the windows."

After a few minutes of quick contortions, they found themselves in a placid stretch of water. But rounding a bend they saw what was obviously one of the huge waterfalls they feared. Half a mile ahead, the stream simply dropped out of sight and they had a clear view down a wide, beautiful valley.

"We've got to get ashore somehow," Nancy called, and she aimed toward the right bank. The water was shallow, but unfortunately there was no place to drive the car completely out of the river and continue overland. The valley walls fell too sharply. The best the travelers could do was to drive it up on a narrow ledge four inches above the water.

"Well, this is it," Nancy said. "Good-bye, good old quiet brown car. We'll have to leave you here."

Ned started to laugh. "This is really terrible, you know. Do you realize how long it's going to be before Herr Gutterman finds his car?"

"Oh, he'll pop up again and we can give him directions," Nancy said, her eyes twinkling.

"We can give him directions, all right, but how will he ever get it out of here?"

"By helicopter," Nancy replied. "A helicopter

could pull him out, and speaking of a helicopter, we could sure use one ourselves."

Night was coming on, and with no way out except straight up the steep side of the valley, the two young people began to lose their jocular mood. The higher they climbed, the more rugged the terrain, and their breathing and luggage became heavier.

At last, after what seemed an interminable length of time, they started downhill again, discovered a path, then a road, and finally a town. As luck would have it, a bus destined for Vienna was due, and ten minutes later, they were standing in the aisle, clinging to the luggage racks for support.

"Look at us," Ned said. "Our feet and our shoes and socks are soaked. We've got mud on our clothes. We've had no lunch or dinner and we have to stand up all the way to Vienna."

But as Ned spoke, two people sitting nearby prepared to get off the bus at the next stop. With relief and soft cries of thanks, the two exhausted young people sank into the empty seats.

"Safe at last," Nancy said.

Suddenly, there was a commotion ahead in the road. "Wait, wait!" came the cry in German. "Wait for us."

Realizing it was Gutterman's voice, Nancy's blood froze. She grabbed Ned's hand and squeezed. "Be quiet," she whispered, hastily pulling two large scarves out of the bag lying at her feet. Quickly, she

90

tied one around her head. "Do you have a hat?" she whispered.

"Yes, my old crushable Irish tweed. Got it in my pocket."

"Put it on your head. I know it's not good manners, but this is an emergency."

Nancy then handed him the second scarf to tie around his neck. She pulled his hat low and adjusted the scarf before they both eased down in their seats, pretending to sleep.

Gutterman and Burger clambered aboard and made their way down the aisle to take positions directly next to the couple.

Gutterman was still in a temper. Burger was sullen. He said nothing while Gutterman sputtered low, threatening sounds, all in German. Nancy, from her limited knowledge of the language, was able to pick out the essence of Herr Gutterman's bitterness. Burger, he said, was to blame for everything. If he had not made iced coffee back in the shepherd's hut, Nancy Drew could never have thrown it in his face and distracted him enough to get out the door.

Then, when he, Herr Gutterman, had bravely put his fist through the door and lain down in front of the wheels, Burger had not had the presence of mind to lie down in back of the wheels, preventing the escape.

And so it went as Nancy listened, her heart beat-

91

ing for fear they would be detected. Still, she could not help but be amused by Herr Gutterman's obvious frustrations. Eventually, Gutterman and Burger obtained seats directly in front of Nancy and Ned, and the two young people sat quietly until they arrived in Vienna. Cautious, they waited for their former captors to disembark before the couple took off their scarves, grabbed their luggage, and caught a taxi for their hotel.

Rooms were waiting for them and because they both felt exhausted, they decided to say good night immediately. Nancy ran a hot tub and was already soaking when she heard the phone ring. Stumbling out of the tub, she wrapped herself in one of the huge European hotel towels and lifted the receiver. It was Ned.

"Nancy!" he cried. "I was watching television, and guess what? We made the headlines! We've been listed as missing. They found the car."

"What?"

"Someone found the car and there are pictures on TV showing it being airlifted by helicopter. Authorities haven't figured out whom it belongs to yet."

"Just wait till they do," Nancy said. "When Gutterman finds out what happened to his car, he'll explode like a volcano!"

"We'd better call Dr. Bagley to tell him we're all right," Ned suggested.

Nancy placed the call to Salzburg instantly. "Professor," she said, "this is Nancy."

There was a stunned silence and then shouts of joy. "Nancy! It's Nancy. Are you all right? Is Ned there? What in the world is going on?"

Quickly, Nancy recounted the kidnapping, the escape, and the crazy fate of Herr Gutterman's car. Professor Bagley agreed that from now on, the tour had to keep close track of everyone.

The professor then filled her in on the group's activities—including the trip to Mozart's birthplace, where the little bus driver was barred from entering. "The authorities there said he always makes a scene and contradicts the guides constantly." The professor laughed.

"Oh, and one other funny thing happened," he added. "Eric left his wheelchair outside the men's room because it wouldn't fit through the door. We lifted him inside and when we came out, he noticed there was a different wheelchair in place of his. Another young man had taken Eric's by mistake, but Eric managed to catch him. For a minute, the other fellow was wheeling his chair like mad, trying to get away because he thought Eric was a little crazy chasing him yelling at the top of his lungs."

Nancy laughed. "That's all we need," she said, "a stolen wheelchair." As she hung up the receiver, she heard a noise that made her whirl around. An envelope suddenly appeared beneath her door. She stepped toward it, feeling her pulse quicken. The envelope was addressed to NANCY DREW, CAR THIEF.

11

Wild-Goose Chase

Without waiting to read the message inside the envelope, Nancy dashed impulsively to the door and flung it wide as she stepped out to see if she could catch a glimpse of the messenger. The corridor was empty.

She smacked her forehead lightly with the palm of her hand. "Oh, that could have been Gutterman," she muttered. "Of course, it was Gutterman. And I opened the door and ran out."

Quickly, she tore open the envelope and read the message written in old-fashioned script.

> *Dear Nancy Drew,*
> *You are to cease all independent efforts to*
> *kidnap the children and to find the film*

Captive Witness. *If you persist, you will be hurt. If the price is right, however, it may be possible for you to obtain both the children and the film. Be in the hotel lobby at 9 P.M. tomorrow. Come alone. I will take you to see the film to prove I have it. You have my word of honor that you will not be harmed. You will be returned safely. Afterward, we can talk about what I really seek from you people.*

G.

So Gutterman does know I'm looking for the film! Nancy said to herself.

Although she had half suspected it, this was the first time he had given any indication of such knowledge, and Nancy concluded that he must have discovered her connection with *Captive Witness* fairly recently. Otherwise, she was sure he would have spoken to her about it long before.

But how did he find out? If her phone call home wasn't tapped, then, Nancy concluded, there must be a spy in the film festival's office who overheard a conversation between Richard Ernst and her father!

The prospects of her meeting with Gutterman churned in her mind as she flopped into bed and fell asleep uneasily.

When she saw Ned the next morning, she said nothing about Gutterman's note or about the invitation to meet him alone that night to see the documentary. It bothered her to keep it secret from Ned, but she believed that the fate of the children and the film hinged on a risk that was solely hers—finding out what Gutterman wanted!

First, she must learn all she could about the stolen film. After brunch, she telephoned the festival office and spoke to Richard Ernst, who her father had said would be her best source of information.

They found the festival offices just off the Ringstrasse, the great band of streets enclosing downtown Vienna which once marked the outer walls where the Turkish invasions had stopped in the sixteenth and again in the seventeenth century.

"Do you know," Nancy asked Ned as their taxi made its way through the crowded streets, "that those sieges of Vienna gave us two things we now eat for breakfast?"

Ned shook his head.

"Well, it was during the first Turkish siege that the bakers of Vienna invented the Vienna roll. And it was the Turks who brought coffee to Central Europe. Can you imagine Europe today without its coffeehouses?"

"And with that colorful information," Ned said, "we find ourselves in front of the film festival offices."

Richard Ernst, the festival representative, was a

meticulously dressed, polite, and proper Austrian who kissed Nancy's hand and offered coffee and delicious pastries. When Nancy asked for milk instead, he smilingly obliged.

But soon his face became serious. "Last Wednesday," Mr. Ernst said, "a man appeared with a letter written on Kurt Kessler's stationery and bearing Mr. Kessler's signature. It instructed festival authorities to give the messenger the copy of *Captive Witness* in our possession and to accept in exchange a revised copy that the messenger handed us."

"I'm surprised there was no more formal procedure involved," Nancy said.

"Well, we winged it, as you Americans say, because it was the first time anything like that had ever happened to us. We're a fairly new festival and, I suppose, a bit naive."

"So you simply gave the man the original film?" Nancy continued.

"No, I left the room to ask my associate, Mr. Etienne, what he thought, and when I came back, I discovered that the messenger had taken our copy and left the so-called revision. It turned out to be a completely blank reel. As I told your father, Miss Drew, we accept full responsibility and we will pay all damages, but I'm sure that money is not the real issue. For Mr. Kessler, it is the heartbreak of losing a vast piece of his lifework."

"Would you describe the man who took the film,"

Nancy requested. "On the other hand, let me. He was short, wiry, with pitted, rather sallow skin. He's almost bald, but not at all well mannered so he probably never removed his hat. He has a kind of ratlike face and beady eyes."

Mr. Ernst gasped. "That's amazing. Miss Drew, I must say I suddenly have enormous respect for your detective abilities."

"I must confess," Nancy replied, "that we've been tangled up with a couple of bad characters for the past few days. The one I described played the role of a bus driver, so why not a messenger, too?"

Nancy paused for a moment, letting her eyes gaze off into space, her brow slightly furrowed. "May I see the can that the film was in when the messenger brought it?"

"The can?" Mr. Ernst asked. "Why, yes, I suppose so."

He rummaged through files and produced a metal can, considerably battered, with some labels still attached. Nancy checked each label. The can had travelled all over Europe: Warsaw, Paris, Berlin, Rome. But there was only one label from Vienna, which she examined closely with her pocket-size magnifying glass.

"This is it! Thank you very much, Mr.—er, Herr Ernst. Come on, Ned."

"Nancy, where are we going? What do you mean, 'this is it'? Will you slow down? Nancy!"

But the girl detective was running now, down the steps, out into the street, signaling for a taxi. Ned caught up in time to open the door for her. When they were both inside, Nancy gave the driver an address she had scribbled down.

The driver glanced back at the two of them. "Are you sure you young people want to go there?" he said in a deep, resonant voice.

"Yes, yes," Nancy said, "and hurry, please."

"Nancy," Ned persisted, "what did you see on that film can?"

"An address of a film company here in Vienna. Chances are that that was the place the blank reel came from and probably the same place where Kessler's copy of *Captive Witness* was taken. Understand?"

"Interesting idea," Ned said, "but it seems a little thin."

"I've had thinner clues," Nancy remarked, settling back to watch the scenery. That proved to be a grim experience, however, as the buildings and the people began to look more disreputable. The road became bumpier, too, more pitted with holes, and littered with debris.

To make matters worse, the afternoon skies had darkened and droplets of rain splashed against the windows. As they passed one corner, a group of street urchins threw stones at the cab.

"Charming section," Nancy told the driver. "I'm

100

hoping it ends before we reach the company office we want. It's called Ciné-Ouest."

When they found Ciné-Ouest, however, it was in a wreck of a building set back from the road and almost concealed by weeds and high bushes. No one seemed to be around. Ned asked the driver to wait.

"Wait? Not a chance. You two young people would be smart to return immediately to your hotel. They'll steal the fillings from your teeth out here."

"We'll be all right," Ned insisted halfheartedly, as they paid the man and stepped out for a look at their target. Wasting no time, the driver locked all the doors, made a U-turn, and sped away in a shower of mud.

Together Nancy and Ned made their way to the front door of Ciné-Ouest. It was locked.

"That figures," Nancy said. "It's Saturday and the employees probably work a five-day week. Let's see if someone left a window open."

"That's burglary, technically speaking, of course."

"I know. But so long as we don't take anything, it's only trespassing," Nancy rationalized. "Besides, if we do find *Captive Witness*, it's our right to take it because it was stolen from our side in the first place."

"Okay, you convinced me." Ned sighed. "Let me try this window."

To his surprise, it opened easily. Both he and

Nancy slipped through onto the first floor, which was surprisingly neat, clean, and well painted. They found themselves in a room with racks and racks of films.

"It'll take hours to go through all this stuff," Ned moaned. "Wouldn't we do better to come back with a court order and some policemen?"

"Uh-uh," Nancy said. "The spy network over here would know in a minute. They'd move the film for sure. No, we just have to start looking."

But before taking another step, they were halted in their tracks by a low, menacing growl. A giant Doberman pinscher guard dog stood thirty feet away with his snout poised low and his lips drawn back exposing great, slashing teeth. He stared at them, ready to pounce.

Almost simultaneously, Nancy and Ned said the identical words: "Don't move and don't breathe."

"Don't look him in the eye, either," Nancy added. "The dog will think you're challenging him and will attack."

"You're probably right," Ned said, "but I have a hunch this guy means to jump us no matter what we do. What about those stacks? Do you think we can climb them fast enough to get away?"

"Yes, but then we'd be stuck there until Monday morning."

"What about your trusty tear-gas book?" Ned asked.

"I have it, but it only works up to about six feet."

"Well, once he's that close, he'll go all the way. Still, give me the book."

"Oh, no," Nancy said. "It's mine. I can handle this as well as you can."

"Maybe so," Ned went on, "but I happen to be standing about two feet in front of you and that means he is going to deal with me first. Please give me the book, Nancy."

"All right, but—"

"Uh-oh!" Ned broke in, snapping up the book. "Here he comes!"

With a savage roar, the giant dog flew across the room in three huge bounds. Nancy was just about to leap toward the window as the dog landed, preparing to spring in a final lunge. Ned, however, sprayed his eyes with tear gas at point-blank range, slightly from the side.

The animal yelped, making Nancy wince as she hurried outside. But she knew that the Doberman, whining now and pawing at his eyes, would not suffer any permanent damage. He would regain full sight within a day.

Meanwhile, Ned had climbed through the window, too. He grabbed Nancy's hand and led her running up the road away from Ciné-Ouest.

After a block, they slowed to a walk. They trudged through the drenching rain for what seemed like hours before finding a cab, and arrived back at the hotel, mud-splattered, soaked to the skin, and exhausted.

"That was wonderful fun." Ned grinned at Nancy. "And we've never looked lovelier. Now, master detective, do you have any more excursions planned for me tonight?"

She was about to say no when nervous thoughts about her nine o'clock meeting with Gutterman began to plague her. Should she tell Ned so that he could shadow her and call in the police if necessary? Or would Ned, in his eagerness to protect her, be discovered? If so, the young detective could lose her only chance to free the children and find the valuable film!

12

Captive Witness

Despite the risk, Nancy decided she had to carry out the mission by herself. She thanked Ned, and with the promise to be up bright and early for breakfast, she parted from him and returned to her room to repair some of the damage to her mud-spattered clothes.

After a hot bath and a hasty manicure, she dressed in a simple navy-blue skirt and white blouse with a powder-blue cardigan.

Gutterman arrived promptly at nine. Burger, of course, was with him, driving a rather battered and old-looking automobile.

"I must apologize for the homely nature of my car, Miss Drew," Herr Gutterman said, "but it

105

seems that magnificent ones attract strange people who borrow and dump them in unlikely places."

Nancy felt her jaw tighten, but she refrained from answering.

"But let bygones be bygones, at least for now," Gutterman said. He smiled thinly. "Would you be so kind as to sit in the back seat with me while Mr. Burger drives? For security reasons, of course."

Nancy nodded. "Do you want to blindfold me, too?"

Gutterman clapped his hands together in an expression of rapture. "How wonderful to do business with a professional! Of course, we must keep the location of this film a secret. *Ja?*"

"*Ja!*" Nancy declared.

Gutterman tied a large, clean white handkerchief around her head. "And now, Miss Drew, I'm sure you are going to try memorizing the sequence of every turn we make. I advise you to save your energy. You'll only get terribly frustrated."

Despite the warning, Nancy tried to note all turns and stops, but the constant twisting made the route nearly impossible to follow.

When the car came to a final halt, Gutterman helped her out and escorted her up a flight of twelve very low steps, leading her through a heavy door that squeaked badly on its hinges. Once inside, they turned right down a short hall and right again through a door that Gutterman closed and locked.

He sat Nancy in a chair and removed her blindfold. They were in a dimly lit room with a film projector behind her and a blank white screen in front of her. Without a word of explanation, Gutterman hit the projection switch, turned off the lights and for one hour, Nancy watched the first part of Kurt Kessler's film, *Captive Witness*.

What passed across the screen was a documentary film of life inside Kessler's homeland. Leading intellectuals, most of them with their backs to the camera, spoke against cruelty and oppression. There were segments showing beatings on the street by police and other unpleasant scenes that created a harrowing image for the oppressed countries of Eastern Europe.

When the reel finished, Gutterman flicked off the switch and turned on the lights. "There is one more piece of film," he said, "but it's a waste of my time to keep watching this drivel. Have you seen enough?"

Nancy, who was greatly moved by what she had seen, looked scornfully at the man. "Yes, thank you. Besides, I'll see the whole thing at the festival."

Gutterman laughed raucously. "You have a delicious sense of humor, Miss Drew. Also a ridiculous sense of honor that actually led you to believe no harm would befall you tonight."

Nancy flashed her eyes. "What?"

"Now, don't get so upset. No harm will come to you tonight, but what astonishes me is that you actually did trust me. Nine times out of ten you would have been wrong."

"Can we get to the point?"

"Oh, by all means. Let's start with my proposition."

"Excuse me," Nancy said. "Let's start with mine. The fact is that none of your people know where the children are. You're bluffing."

A glimmer of annoyance crossed Gutterman's face. He waggled one thick forefinger at Nancy. "Don't get cute with me, Miss Drew. We not only know where they are but who kidnapped them from us as well as the precise date and time they will try to escape.

"We will be there to intercept all of them, unless, of course, you are reasonable." Gutterman rubbed his hands together and walked away a few paces, glancing back at Nancy dramatically. "All we want is the arch traitor, Kurt Kessler! The man who turned on his own country and who now desires to show this treacherous film about his own people! It's a lie—all of it!"

Nancy flared up. "Kurt Kessler happens to be one of the most respected film directors in the entire world. I'm sure he must be telling the truth, and if he isn't, then why doesn't your government refute him with facts and logic instead of punishing help-less children?"

A small smile played around Gutterman's lips. "Did you say *my* government? Miss Drew, I have no ideology. I am a patriot who pledges allegiance to whoever pays me the most. If, after you give me Kurt Kessler, your country wishes to buy my services, I might even steal him back for you!"

"I don't think we'd ever sink that low!" Nancy replied scathingly.

Gutterman waved his hand, carelessly dismissing the insult. "You can't hurt my feelings, Miss Drew. I abandoned them years ago. Now, what have you decided? Will you persuade Kessler to appear at the border crossing and give himself up? As I said, you can have the children and even this silly film, because they will make him renounce it. He will say the Americans made him do it."

Nancy tried to conceal her revulsion, knowing that the success of her mission relied partly on Gutterman.

"You mean," she said, her voice trembling with outrage, "that you will torture him until he denies everything he believes in? Haven't you done enough to him already? You made him spend nine years in labor camps and four years under house arrest, and what about all the other years when his work was confiscated or destroyed?"

"I've no time for your nonsense," Gutterman

said, replacing her blindfold. "I want you to contact Kessler. Let him make his own decision. You have until noon tomorrow."

In a dazzling series of twists and turns, the young detective was returned to the hotel. She immediately went to a pay phone and called her father, relating Gutterman's offer. Mr. Drew put her on hold while he contacted Kessler and then came back to Nancy with the answer.

"Of course," Carson Drew said, his voice crackling with anger, "I knew what Kurt would say. He's a hero, and heroes automatically do things like this. You tell your contact that Mr. Kessler will fly to Vienna tomorrow. He will do as they request on a guarantee there will be no tricks, Nancy."

As her father finished speaking, tears flowed down Nancy's cheeks, and she had a hard time keeping her voice from breaking. "Okay, Dad. No tricks, and tell Mr. Kessler we all love him."

Nancy went to her room, changed out of her clothes into a nightgown and stared dazedly in a mirror as she brushed her hair. The sorrow over Kessler's probable fate, however, soon replaced itself with anger.

"Wait a minute," Nancy murmured out loud. "If only I could retrace the route to the building where *Captive Witness* was stored!"

She knew she couldn't possibly recall the twisting, winding way but there were other things that came to mind. The sounds, for example. She had heard trains coupling and uncoupling and there had been the shriek of a train whistle. From somewhere, too, had come the music of a merry-go-round. Where in all Vienna would that be? She had less than two days to find out!

For several moments, too, the young detective thought of the ten children in hiding. How much longer would they remain safe from the other side?

13

The Stricken Messenger

After a full night's sleep, Nancy bounced out of bed filled with energy. She couldn't be sure of the route Gutterman's car had taken her, but she had jotted down everything she could remember.

She dialed Ned's room number and was greeted by his sleepy voice. "Come on, Ned. Get up and get dressed. Meet me right way. We've no time to lose. Today is the big day! Breakfast in ten minutes."

Half an hour later, Ned, still bleary-eyed, wandered into the hotel restaurant and slid into the seat opposite Nancy. "I can't believe it." He yawned. "You look radiant and I look like a sack of wet laundry. How do you do it, Nancy?"

Nancy waved her hand impatiently and grinned.

"Now stop flattering me and be serious. Look." She pushed a map of Vienna toward him. It was cross-hatched with lines of purple, green, and red.

"What is this?" Ned mumbled, taking a swig of orange juice.

"It's the route to the film," Nancy said.

"Which film? Our film—*Captive Witness?*"

"Yes, yes, yes. I saw part of it last night."

Ned was completely confused. "Last night?"

The girl shook her head. "I saw it with Gutterman."

"Gutterman!" Ned exclaimed.

"I wish you'd stop repeating everything I say." Nancy laughed.

"Well, everything you say is so fascinating I just can't help myself."

"Let me explain," Nancy said, and told her friend the entire story of her meeting with the man.

"That's really terrific," Ned said when she had finished. "I came along to protect you and what do you do? Play right into the hands of that crook."

"But I had to. Don't you see? If I had told you, they might have found out and canceled the whole thing. I'm sorry. Forgive me. But please hurry. I need you to rent and drive a car so we can retrace the route Gutterman took me on last night."

Ned looked at her ruefully for a moment, then smiled. "Okay. Let's go."

Once they had secured a car and were on their way, Nancy spread the map on her lap. "I think it was somewhere around here."

Ned paused to follow her finger. "You realize, of course, you're pointing to half of Vienna," he said.

"I know." Nancy sighed. "Well, let's start with the red line, and keep our speed at twenty miles per hour."

For more than four hours, they cruised up one street and down another with no success. At last, Nancy folded up the map and put it in the glove compartment.

"I give up," she said.

"Oh, don't do that," Ned replied.

"But it's hopeless. I didn't see any building with a flight of twelve very low steps leading up to the front door."

"Shall we go back then?"

Nancy nodded grimly.

"Look, it isn't worth fretting over. You did better today than yesterday. At least, this time we didn't get chased by a hungry Doberman."

"Thanks for the consolation," Nancy said, half-smiling.

They returned to the hotel in time to meet Professor Bagley and their friends who were arriving on the tour bus. The first voice they heard was that of the little bus driver. It was loud and strident, commanding the attention of everyone within a block.

114

"Strauss! Oh yes, he was so-so. He wrote pretty music—*The Blue Danube* and *Tales from the Vienna Woods*. But what is that compared to Mozart?"

Suddenly, Bess and George spotted Nancy coming toward them. "Nancy!" the cousins chimed simultaneously and raced toward her.

"I see our bus driver is still at it." Nancy grinned.

"All the way from Salzburg." George groaned.

"Did he run off the road again?"

"Not once but many times," Bess said. "It was awful. Once he got so angry because someone compared Beethoven to Mozart that he actually stopped the bus, ran outside, and shouted into the valley, 'Beethoven is a bore. Mozart is sublime.' Over and over. The professor had to go out and drag him back into the bus."

As soon as Nancy had seen Bess and George off to their rooms, she turned to Professor Bagley and the ever-present Eric Nagy. They went to a nearby sidewalk café, and after ordering hot chocolate and croissants with butter and jam, Nancy related her recent experiences, including the fact that Kessler would probably agree to trade himself for the ten children.

Dr. Bagley's face drained white. "We can't let that happen," he said angrily. "Kessler can't go back."

"I know," Nancy said under her breath. "Have

you received your final instructions regarding the time and place of the crossing?"

"Not a word, but I expect to receive information today. I've been told to stay around the hotel and keep myself visible. By the way, the cat burgler struck at last."

Nancy's eyes twinkled with excitement. "You mean they took the bait?"

"They certainly did. Last night, I left the false document in a sealed envelope at the bottom of my musette bag. I had folded the message twice and dropped a few grains of salt in the middle of it. This morning, I opened the envelope and the salt was gone. Someone did an excellent job of unsealing the envelope, reading the contents, and resealing it perfectly, but didn't notice the salt."

"Well, I must say that was a bit more subtle than the business at Munich airport," Nancy remarked. "Of course, I suppose if the theft had worked there, you probably would've found the bag later, thrown away somewhere, with certain things missing but the envelope left intact just to make it look like a regular robbery."

"Good deduction, but that would have been equally clumsy of them. Anyway, now that they have the information, all we have to do is wait for our contact to surface with the correct details."

Ned, who had gone to his room, returned shortly

to join them, engaging in banter with Eric as they vied for Nancy's attention. Dr. Bagley watched in amusement wearing his owl look.

Suddenly, Nancy heard a man's voice coming from the table directly behind the professor. "Don't turn around, Dr. Bagley," he said softly, but urgently. "Pretend I'm not here. I am your contact. Listen carefully. We are now free to tell you where you will find the true instructions regarding the rendezvous with the children. Look—"

The voice stopped, choking in a half-strangled sound. Nancy whirled out of her chair to see the man fall in the throes of a heart seizure. She took the initiative, helping Ned and the professor roll the man on his back and loosen his clothes. Leaning on her extensive training in first aid and paramedic techniques, she took his pulse and bent to listen for his heartbeat.

"I don't hear anything," she cried.

Quickly, she assumed the correct position for mouth-to-mouth resuscitation while Ned, who had assisted Nancy in similar emergencies, administered chest pounding.

In seconds, the man was breathing again and his heart began to beat. "Keep him warm," Nancy ordered as some hotel employees appeared with a blanket. "I hope that someone has called an ambulance."

Indeed, someone had, and as they waited for its arrival, the victim began to regain consciousness though he was paralyzed on the left side of his body.

He tried to speak but could make only indistinct, gurgling sounds. Nancy tried to quiet him, but his eyes rolled wildly toward Eric Nagy.

"What's he trying to tell us?" Dr. Bagley said anxiously.

But the man's words were so garbled, neither Nancy, Ned, Eric, nor the professor could decipher them.

"It's a shame," Nancy said as the ambulance came. The man tried to raise himself, pointing at Eric before falling back on the stretcher, exhausted. "I know he's trying to tell us something about Eric, but what?" the girl muttered.

"I have no idea," Dr. Bagley whispered back, "but it's impossible to discuss secret business with fifty people gaping over our shoulders."

"Someone ought to stay with him every single minute until he's able to communicate," Nancy remarked.

"I agree, but I don't think—" the professor started to say as the doctor in charge interrupted the conversation.

He complimented Nancy and her friends for saving the man's life while attendants carefully placed the patient in the ambulance.

"Thank you," Nancy said. "I'm his niece and I would like to accompany him if I may."

Ned gasped and the professor looked up, somewhat less startled.

"I'll call you from the hospital," the young detective told her companions as the ambulance doors closed and the vehicle moved off.

What no one had noticed, however, was the small, black car that had pulled away from the curb and followed the ambulance. In the front seat with evil grins on their faces were Herr Gutterman and Herr Burger.

14

The Terrible Truth

In the ambulance, Nancy looked through the man's
wallet for some clue regarding his identity, so that
should he die, contact might be made with the people who had sent him. His name was Robert Haberman and his address was in West Berlin. That was
the only information Nancy found.

At the hospital, after a prolonged examination,
the doctors told Nancy that Herr Haberman was doing fine, that the paralysis was only temporary and
he would soon recover.

Nancy begged to stay at his bedside because it
was important for her to speak with him, if only for a
few seconds, when he regained his speech or could
hold a pencil to write a message. The doctor agreed,

and Nancy sat quietly next to Herr Haberman's bed.

"I admire you, Herr Robert Haberman," Nancy said softly. "But how I wish you would wake up soon."

Remembering her promise to call Professor Bagley and Ned, she stepped into the corridor but froze instantly at the sight of Herr Gutterman arguing with a hospital guard.

"But he is my brother," Gutterman was pleading.

Nancy hesitated. "That man is not related to us at all," she declared, hurrying forward to confront Gutterman.

"*Related to us?*" Gutterman bellowed. "See here, my good fellow, this woman is not related to that patient at all!"

"I bet he can't tell you his brother's name," Nancy said quickly, watching Gutterman flounder.

"All right," the guard said, "what is his name?"

"He uses many names," Gutterman went on. "His real name is Gutterman, of course."

"That's enough," the guard replied, taking Herr Gutterman by the arm and twisting his wrist just enough to keep him under control. "Now, please leave this hospital."

With Gutterman out of the way, at least for the moment, Nancy dashed to a public phone and called the professor's room. Ned answered.

"We're all sitting here trying to figure out what to do. Did our friend revive?"

"No," Nancy said, "but he'll be all right, thank goodness. I'm afraid, though, he might not be able to talk to us for days, and we don't have that much time. Also, Gutterman's been trying to force his way in here. I got rid of him for a little while but I wouldn't be surprised if he doesn't blow everything for us."

"Well, something's got to give. Wait. The professor wants to talk with you."

"Hello, Nancy,"

"Hello, Dr. Bagley. Do you have any ideas what we should do next?"

"Not really. I was hoping our contact man had a backup who would fill in for him in case something unexpected like this happened. No luck, though. We did have another strange incident, too. Somebody went off with Eric's wheelchair. This time it wasn't by mistake. He actually tried to steal it."

"What?"

"It's true. Somebody grabbed it and tried to get out the front door with it, but the doorman's pretty tough. When he went after the thief, well, the fellow let go of the chair and just ran."

"Did you see him?"

"No. And the doorman couldn't give much of a description either."

Suddenly, bells began tripping off in Nancy's head. Eric's wheelchair! When Herr Haberman suffered his attack, he kept looking at Eric, trying to point to him, to say something. But what?

"Ned!" Nancy cried. "Go straight to Eric. Guard him. Guard that wheelchair—with your life if necessary. Forget about sending anybody to this hospital to relieve me. I'm coming right back."

She raced past the friendly guard, almost knocking him down in her haste and calling an apology at the same time, and headed outside. She leaped into a cab and begged the driver to take her to the hotel as fast as the speed limit allowed. Once there, she ignored the stately, lumbering elevators and flew up the three flights of stairs to the professor's door.

Ned called out. "Who's there?"

"Me!" she panted. "Let me in, please."

As soon as she was inside, she rushed toward Eric. "Please, can you get out of your wheelchair and sit on the bed for a while?" Nancy requested.

When the young man complied, she asked Ned to find some tools, including a screwdriver, pliers, and a hammer. "Oh, yes, and order another wheelchair right away."

"Nancy," Dr. Bagley said, moving toward her, "you're going too fast for all of us. Slow down, and tell us what you're up to."

Nancy pointed to Eric's chair eagerly. "The message must be hidden in there—all the instructions for rescuing the children. We've been carrying the information ever since we left the States, but they didn't want us or the enemy to know."

As the young detective's revelation settled on everyone, all three men responded with equal excitement. Tools and a substitute wheelchair were ordered promptly, and the professor and Eric began fiddling with the metal frame, trying to unscrew the bolts with their bare hands.

Within ten minutes, the entire chair had been stripped down to its components. Even the rubber had been removed from the wheels on the chance the instructions were concealed underneath. But they weren't. Despite all their efforts, there was no trace of anything.

Nancy clapped her hands to her forehead, holding them there in frustration. "Oh, I feel so foolish, and I was so positive!"

"Don't blame yourself, Nancy," Dr. Bagley comforted her. "We all thought you were on the right track."

"But now poor Mr.—I mean, Herr—Haberman is still the only one who can help us. Somebody should go back and stand guard again."

"I'll do it," Ned offered.

"Just a minute, Ned," Eric said, clearing his throat. "I've been thinking about the wheelchair seat. I noticed a little while ago that it's slightly uncomfortable. As a matter of fact, there's a tiny lump in it."

He pointed to the leather seat, which had been cut off the chair but otherwise lay intact on the floor.

"The seat!" Nancy cried. "Oh, of course! I could kiss you, Eric!"

"Better not," Ned replied in a half-kidding tone. "But somebody had better open that seat. Here, let me."

Taking out his penknife, Ned inserted the blade in the leather seam, slitting the stitches holding the two pieces together. Out fell a small, thick brown envelope.

Nancy tore open the flap and then quickly handed the packet to the professor. Dr. Bagley adjusted his glasses and started to read. He became so engrossed in the message that he forgot to read it aloud. Instead, he stood there, mumbling softly under his breath, making little exclamations while the three young people swelled with curiosity.

Suddenly, Dr. Bagley looked up, aware of his oversight, and apologized profusely. "Oh, I'm terribly sorry. This is so fascinating," he said. "The plan is to let our enemies think the crossing will be made on the Czech frontier while in fact the children will be escaping over the Hungarian border.

"There is a small, detailed map here that indicates the exact place between Austria and Hungary where the children will be brought and from which the final move will be accomplished."

Everyone was jubilant. "If we can just get those kids out safely," Ned said, "it will be worth the whole expedition. Of course, it would be super if Nancy could find the *Captive Witness* film, too. But the main issue is those kids and saving Mr. Kessler from a fate worse than death."

Nancy remained quiet on the subject, though deep down it saddened her to think she might fail to recover the film. After all, it represented something very important to its creator.

As she pondered the idea, a knock on the door interrupted. It was a soft, insistent knock that somehow made everyone feel there was something urgent waiting on the other side.

Professor Bagley opened the door and found himself looking down at a short, frightened-looking man. He stood alone with his hat held diffidently in his hand.

"You are Dr. Bagley?" the visitor said softly, taking a quick glance down the corridor to make sure no one had followed him.

The professor nodded.

"May I come in? I have very important news. Terrible news."

Hurriedly, the professor ushered him in and then closed and locked the door. The stranger stood uncomfortably in the middle of the room. He was obviously poor and bedraggled but had done his best to make himself presentable enough to enter the hotel. His graying hair had been combed into place, but his pants bagged and his old coat was shiny with the memory of such hard use.

Even though he's bone dry, Nancy thought, he looks like a shivering puppy.

The man sat down gently as though fearful he would break something. He looked from one to another seeking permission to speak further. Nancy nodded her head encouragingly and he began.

"My name is Emile Popov. We had hoped to bring ten children out through Hungary with six adults posing as three married couples traveling with their children. We picked Hungary because it is so much easier to cross the border there. The Hungarians and Austrians are on good terms unless, of course, an alert is sounded.

"Of course, with our enemies looking for the children, we have to expect the Hungarians to tighten their security, too.

"Even so, we thought we could do it until two of our couples were arrested while traveling from East Germany. My wife and I managed to escape, thank goodness. We have all the children and we arrived this morning at a little hut. It's almost a dugout, hidden in the brush about a mile from the border in the swampy section of the lake.

"But we now have no way to get across. We can't try to go through the regular checkpoint with ten children. We can't expect to climb the fence at some other point along the border. Our organization has been disrupted. Almost everyone has been arrested or gone into hiding."

"Mr. Popov," Professor Bagley said, "what do you propose we do?"

"With God's help, Professor Bagley," the man said, "you must find a way to sneak some people across the border, pick up our children, and come back here with them. We have no one left to do the job."

15

Perilous Plan

As Professor Bagley heard the little man's words, he shook his head. "I think," he said, "I'd better sit down." He sank heavily into a great brown armchair and stared at the floor.

Nancy, on the other hand, decided that their visitor needed some cheering up. "Well, Mr. Popov, how would you like something to eat? It's time to relax a bit, and when we're all done talking, you should have a bath and then a bed because I can see that you've had to do some crawling and hiding to get here. Am I right?"

Mr. Popov nodded somberly. He looked down at his hands, which Nancy had noticed were badly scratched, with flakes of dirt around the nails. His shoes were muddy, too.

"With your permission, dear lady," he said, "I gratefully accept the offer. Food and a bath would be wonderful. But first, let me at least wash my hands and face."

He disappeared into the bathroom while Nancy phoned room service and the young men donated slacks, a shirt, and a jacket to replace Mr. Popov's tattered clothing.

Professor Bagley stared at Nancy, still perplexed. "I didn't expect this at all. Really I didn't. We're not equipped to go into Hungary. I don't know how we would start. The refugee organization shouldn't leave us hanging this way. I mean, I know we have to do something, but—"

Nancy patted his arm. "Why don't we have a long talk with Mr. Popov and try to find out as much about the operation as possible."

"Let's call the refugee organization, too," Dr. Bagley said, brightening at the idea. "You never lose your optimism, do you?"

"Not if I can possibly help it," the girl said.

Professor Bagley dialed the contact for the refugee organization and talked for nearly five minutes.

"There's a storm watch here," he said into the phone. "The wind could start whipping up in a few hours, you know."

Nancy had overheard the tail end of the conversation and was bewildered by the strange talk about bad weather.

"I heard we're due to have clear skies tomorrow," she commented when the professor hung up.

"Storm watch means time is running out," he replied grimly, explaining that he frequently used weather terms as a code. "We can never be sure if someone is listening in on a conversation."

He paused sadly, then added, "They say they're a small group and everyone who works with them is completely committed to two other operations tomorrow. One is on the East German border and the other on the Romanian border. There isn't a person to spare. If only we could hold off our rescue for a week. Let's see what Mr. Popov thinks."

When the man emerged, face and hands now shining, he was overwhelmed by the gifts of clothes laid out for him and the dinner that room service wheeled in moments later. As he ate, Nancy and the professor carefully learned as much as they could about the children, their exact location, their individual ages, and their ability to remain silent when necessary.

"They must keep quiet when they pass close to the Hungarian border guards," the professor told Popov.

"Of course. No question about that, and they will," the man replied. "They understand the seriousness of all this, and they dearly want to be with their families again."

The conversation then shifted to the choice of time selected for the border crossing. It was to have been just before midnight when the guards would be awaiting relief, and when they were apt to be most careless, tired, and eager to get home.

"They would not search so thoroughly then as they would at the beginning of their watch," Mr. Popov said. "But why are we even talking about such things? They are no longer important since there is no way to bring the children out now through a border checkpoint."

"What about the possibility of cutting through the fence?" Ned asked.

Nancy shook her head. "It's probably wired."

"You mean it will electrocute on contact," Ned commented.

"I don't know about that, but I imagine it must be connected to an alarm," Nancy replied.

"How about digging under the fence then?" Eric questioned.

"Friends." Mr. Popov held up his hands to interrupt the discussion. "You can cut the fence. You can dig under. But the risk is so terribly great that the guards would catch you. Remember, with ten children you cannot move very quickly. No, we must think of something completely different."

There was silence until Ned snapped his fingers. "I've heard of people escaping by balloon," he said eagerly, but seeing the frowning faces of his listeners, he dropped the idea. "Where are we going to get a balloon anyhow?"

Nancy studied Mr. Popov for a moment. She was startled to see tears in his eyes. She hurried to his side and put her arm around his thin shoulders. "I am so afraid," Mr. Popov said, half choking, "that I will never see my wife or the children again. It is only a matter of days, perhaps hours, before they find us."

Nancy felt tears spring to her own eyes as she hugged the man encouragingly. "Mr. Popov, you are one of the bravest people I've ever known because you are afraid, but you do what you have to anyway. You have to fight twice—once against your fear and once against your enemy. You are a remarkable man, and we are proud to help you."

Mr. Popov squared his shoulders and said in his still-choking voice, "Thank you, Miss Drew. Thank you."

"And don't worry," Nancy continued, "because we will be there to get you—all of you—tomorrow night."

Professor Bagley gulped. "Ah, Nancy, I'm not sure we should make such a flat promise like that one. We might find it too hard to keep."

"Trust me, Dr. Bagley," the young detective said. "I have a plan. It's not complete yet. But I know it will work." She looked at him imploringly.

At last the professor gave way, and she smiled a little.

"Who can resist you, Nancy? Okay, let's give your plan a chance—particularly since I don't have one of my own."

The girl inhaled deeply. "So far," she said, "only the four of us know about the children. Right?"

"Right," Eric replied.

"Well, we're going to need assistance. We have to bring in Bess, George, Dave, and Burt."

Nancy ran her hand through her hair and paced back and forth. "For now, Mr. Popov, you stay here in this room and we'll ask the hotel to bring in a cot. Okay, Dr. Bagley and Eric?"

They nodded.

"Thank you," Mr. Popov replied. "I am very tired, but I must be up by two A.M. and on my way back so that I can cross before daylight."

"That's fine," Nancy said. "We'll send you along with a duck call. Ned, we must find a duck call."

"A duck call?" the young man said in amazement. "What in the world are you going to do with that?"

"We'll use it for a signal. Get two duck calls. Tomorrow night Mr. Popov will listen for it. When he hears it, he'll answer us. Just three short bursts. Quack! Quack! Quack! That's all. It will be a new moon and black as pitch so it's the only way we'll be able to find one another."

"Besides, it's a natural sound and won't arouse

135

suspicion," Professor Bagley remarked.

"Or not much, I hope," Nancy said.

"The call's a good idea," Mr. Popov concurred. "The place we're staying in isn't a house. It isn't even a hovel. Just a hut. And we have no lights. Even if we did, we couldn't show them."

"Wait a minute, Nancy," the professor interjected. "We have to start thinking about what is physically possible. Now, you know I can't really run. My left leg has been stiff ever since they flattened me for doing that column of music criticism for the River Heights newspaper."

The young people laughed at the professor's habit of making a joke about the wound he had received in combat.

"So," Dr. Bagley continued, "that means I'm going to be kind of a fifth wheel in this operation."

"Not really," Nancy replied. "You are the most visible one. You are the person the other side has been watching most. That could prove to be a very valuable asset."

"You mean I could be your decoy."

"Yes, you and Eric could draw attention away from the real rescue attempt while the rest of us waltz across the border with the Popovs and the children."

Professor Bagley pulled his ear thoughtfully. "Well," he said, "I wouldn't include Eric as a decoy.

In fact, my boy, I think it's time to say something, don't you?"

"Guess so." The young man smiled from his position on bed where he'd been sitting ever since his wheelchair was destroyed. "You and Ned had better sit down when I tell you this, or rather when I show you this."

Nancy furrowed her brow slightly. "Have you some secret weapon that will help us save the children?"

"Oh, just a small one. Here—watch."

The handsome young man stood up and walked across the room in front of the onlookers. For a moment, everyone was speechless, and then recovering, they cried out almost in unison:

"Eric! You can walk!"

16

The Shoppers' Ploy

"Eric!" Nancy cried happily, "you can walk! How wonderful!" And impulsively, she gave him a hug. Ned, too, leaped up and grabbed the boy in a bear hug, slapping him on the back.

"You rascal!" the young collegian said. "You had me fooled, that's for sure."

"Me, too," Nancy said, her eyes sparkling like blue diamonds. "He really is an actor. All I can say is congratulations on your amazing recovery. No doubt you'll have to do a lot more acting if we're going to transport those children safely into Austria. I guess we all will."

"I'm really sorry to have deceived everyone," Eric said, chuckling a little, "but you can see the advantage of my being in a wheelchair. A man who

can't walk wouldn't be of much help to anyone trying to escape enemy territory."

"So our opponents don't regard you as a threat,"
Nancy said.

"And the idea of using the wheelchair to deliver
the final, secret instructions was a stroke of genius,"
Dr. Bagley remarked. "The papers were probably
slipped into the chair that time we lost sight of it in
the hotel."

Once the effect of the surprise had died down,
Nancy and the professor began the complicated
work of organizing a job for each person. First, Nancy telephoned Bess, George, Burt, and Dave and
asked them to join the group.

"Wow, look at that wheelchair," Dave said. "Did
a truck run over it?"

"What on earth happened?" Bess chimed in.

"Everybody sit down and listen," Dr. Bagley told
them. "Please keep your voices down because what
you are about to learn has already set off one explosion in this room. It's amazing all of Vienna didn't
hear it."

In a few sentences, the professor revealed that
Eric could, indeed, walk and the entire group had
to collaborate in an effort to help ten children escape from Eastern Europe. Nancy then filled in
about the missing film and how the enemy had offered to trade it and the children in return for Kurt
Kessler's surrender.

"What?" George said. "That's downright outrageous!"

"I'll say it is!" Bess exclaimed.

Burt and Dave also expressed anger when they heard Nancy's final piece of information.

"Please, please," Dr. Bagley said, quieting the group. "I know how you all must feel but we must keep cool."

"Or we'll ruin everything," Nancy added.

George's eyes flashed fire. "I'll fight them myself," she muttered evenly.

"You bet—me, too," Bess added.

Everyone smiled at this unexpected sign of pugnacity from the usually timid girl.

"Don't look at me that way. I'm an absolute terror when I get angry."

With the preliminary talk behind them, Nancy cleared a large table, spread out a map of the border area, and began marking the points gleaned from the small map found in the wheelchair. She circled the general border area and with Mr. Popov's aid, located the exact spot where the children and Mrs. Popov were hidden.

"It's so close to the border," the man said, "that we thought of making a run for it in the dark, but that would be too much for the smaller children. We'd be sure to make some noise and be discovered in no time."

His listeners fell silent as they considered alternatives. Finally, Nancy tapped her finger on the map and spoke musingly.

"I think I know how to make this whole thing work. Ned, you organize the gang to buy the things I'm going to write down on this list. Then give me some time to make a few phones calls from the booth in the lobby so they can't be traced. We'll meet here in this room at eight o'clock tonight. In the meantime, Mr. Popov, you go to bed and get some sleep."

Nancy's friends read her shopping list with amusement and numerous wisecracks. The list included the following items:

> *Eleven inner tubes*
> *One small tank of compressed air*
> *Black greasepaint*
> *Theatrical makeup kit*
> *One ball gown circa 1880 with hat to match*
> *One titian wig (long hair)*
> *Six assorted pairs of sunglasses*
> *A limousine, but no driver, to be ready at 7 A.M. the next day*
> *A rental car large enough for six people also ready at 7 A.M.*
> *Two duck calls*

Two rubber scuba suits
Detailed maps of the Czech and Hungar-
   ian borders
A chauffeur's uniform to fit Eric
A baseball hat to fit Dave

"Sounds wonderful, but where am I going to find a baseball hat in Vienna?" Dave asked.

"And the titian wig," George said. "Are we going into our sister routine, Nancy?"

"I like the eleven inner tubes and the duck calls." Ned laughed. "Can you fathom what'll happen to me when I stroll into an Austrian department store and ask for eleven inner tubes, two duck calls, and six pairs of sunglasses? They'll haul out a straitjacket!"

"I'll take full responsibility if they do!" Nancy giggled.

"You will?" Ned smiled.

"Of course. Now hurry and try to be back here by eight P.M. for a briefing."

As the group started to leave, Ned halted them. "Hold it a minute. Nancy, come here. Look, quick!"

Nancy ran to the window and peered through the draperies. Below, parked on the other side of the street, was a large, light-blue car.

The girl stared inquiringly at Ned. "What am I supposed to be looking at?"

"In the car," Ned said. "In the passenger seat in front. Do you see him?"

Nancy glanced again. This time she felt a lump in her throat. Herr Gutterman, dressed in a suit that matched the color of the car, had curled his lips into an evil smile and was blowing kisses toward the window.

17

Freedom Props

"Well," Nancy said, "it's Herr Gutterman, but what else is new except the pretty paint job on his sedan?"

"He obviously doesn't care if we see him," Ned said.

"No," Nancy replied, "but that's because he must have a lot of his people staked out around here ready to trail us wherever we go. You realize what that means."

"As we go shopping, we'll have to break up. Each of us will have to head for a different store," Ned said.

"Try to lose them and don't let them see what you're buying. That's important."

The group split up as directed and Nancy retired

to the lobby phone booth with a handful of coins. In quick succession, she called her father, the River Heights Footlighters Club, which was a little theater group, and finally, an old friend of Mr. Drew's, a prominent and wealthy Austrian.

When Nancy emerged from the booth almost an hour later, she was amused by the sight of a somewhat nervous man with square features and thinning hair who pretended to read a newspaper. It took little imagination to see that he was one of Gutterman's henchmen.

Unable to resist the temptation to create some mischief for her enemy's benefit, Nancy ducked back into the phone booth where she hunted for odd telephone numbers. They included the Animal Rescue League, an insect exterminating company, the backstage number of the Opera House, a plumbing supply store, and finally some random names and numbers picked from the directory.

She wrote them down with great care, then crumpled the paper and stuffed it into the top of her bag, allowing it to protrude. Then she stepped out of the phone booth, and walking fast, brushed against a palm branch which caused the paper to rustle to the floor.

As she reached the elevator, she took out her makeup mirror and, pretending to arrange her hair, watched the man with the square face quickly snatch up the paper.

Nancy smiled. That would keep him occupied for most of the afternoon. He'll drive himself crazy looking for the significance behind that jumble of totally meaningless numbers, she mused.

By eight o'clock, most of the group had reassembled in Dr. Bagley's room and Mr. Popov was emerging from a nap, shower, and shave. The luxury of wearing clean clothes added a flush of happiness to his face.

The last of the team to arrive was Bess. She was gasping for breath and dragging a large box. "Never," she said, exaggerating her breathing for comic effect, "never send a girl out to buy an 1880 ball gown in Vienna. Do you know how much it cost? Even to rent? Do you know how much it weighs? I'll tell you. Five hundred pounds, minimum. Feel this thing."

She heaved the large box up on the bed and Nancy, opening the package, held up a long, beautiful red gown.

"Perfect," she said. "Beautiful. Well done, Private Marvin. We might promote you to corporal for this."

"Don't do me any favors," Bess said, laughing, "unless you assign a captain to go with me next time to carry the heavy stuff."

Nancy ran a check on all the items she had requested. With only a few substitutions, her friends had produced everything.

146

"All right, Nancy," Dr. Bagley said, "we've followed your instructions. Now we're eager to hear what you have in mind. Obviously, water is involved. But how?"

"Let's take it step by step," Nancy said. "Professor Bagley will lead the first platoon north, here." She pointed to the map. "This is the Czech border, the place the children are supposed to cross according to the phony documents the enemy has already seen."

"So you think that's where Gutterman's gang will be," Ned said.

"I'd like to believe that, but they may not be there. After all, they were trying awfully hard to get a look at Eric's wheelchair also. They were probably the ones who tried to switch his wheelchair for another one. Who knows what they know by now."

"My group is the decoy, right?" Dr. Bagley said.

"Yes. You will leave in the big rental car pretty early and head for the Czech border, the point I still have my finger on. Don't hurry, though. I think it would be fun if you were to drive all over Vienna first. Do some sightseeing, visit the Vienna Woods, have lunch, and generally drive Gutterman's men crazy. They will never be able to figure out what you're doing. Sound reasonable?"

"Uh-huh," Ned said. "But what about the wig, the inner tubes, and the makeup?"

"Aha," Nancy cried, "that's still a secret. Now,

147

the new wheelchair will be occupied not by Mr. Nagy, but by Mr. Eddleton."

"Me?" Burt gulped. "Why me?"

Nancy grinned. "You're about the same build, almost the same height. You don't really look alike, but you have the same coloring. Now, why don't you try out the chair for size and comfort?"

She led the boy to it, stuck sunglasses on him as well as the baseball cap. Burt smiled broadly.

"How do I look?" he asked.

"Just like a revised edition of Eric Nagy!"

"Ah, please don't praise me too much or it will go to my head."

"So long as you don't lose it," George muttered under her breath.

"Now, George." Nancy smiled. "For one day only, you will be Nancy Drew!"

"Not the famous detective?" Her friend gasped in pretended surprise.

"You will wear this titian wig after we shape it a little bit to look more like my hair."

"Do I get to wear sunglasses, too?" George inquired.

"Of course, and this beautiful, floppy straw hat that will hide most of your face."

"Fantastic," George replied. "And, of course, I will also get to wear your gorgeous white dress. But suppose it doesn't turn out to be a sunny day? Suppose we go mushing up to the Czechoslovakian border and it's raining cats and dogs, and you can hardly see your hand in front of your face. Do we still keep wearing our sunglasses?"

"Mm-hmm. Besides, it won't matter very much," Nancy said, tapping George's head affectionately, "because no one will see you that close up."

"Only when Nancy and I get cornered by a Doberman pinscher," Ned said.

"And Mr. Nickerson," Nancy continued. "How would you like to accompany George in your most attentive manner. You know, stick close and block the enemy's view as much as possible?"

"Oh, so I get to wear sunglasses, too," the boy responded.

"Now let's get down to serious business," Nancy said.

"What about us?" Bess asked, referring to herself and Dave. "Do we turn into wallflowers for the day?"

"Most definitely not. You go along with the gang to the Czech border. Just be your own sweet selves. No disguises necessary."

"Oh, phooey," Bess said, "and I wanted to dress up."

"Why don't you give her an inner tube and some sunglasses, Nancy?" Ned laughed, prompting Nancy to throw a wad of paper at him.

"I'd like to remind everyone that another person will be making the trip to the Czech border and unless our mission succeeds, he won't be coming back."

"You're speaking of Kurt Kessler," Eric said softly.

A hush fell over the group and all joking stopped.

"We have to think of him and those kids at all times," Nancy said. "There's a heavy responsibility weighing on all of us."

"You've explained the decoy operation adequately," the professor said. "But what about the actual rescue of the children? No one has been left unaccounted for except you and Eric."

"And we're the ones who will have to get the children out," Nancy declared.

"Nancy," Ned said with alarm in his voice, "you can't do this by yourselves. You'll need help."

Of course, it wasn't only the awareness of impending danger that had prompted the remark. Ned was also cognizant of his handsome young rival who would be working closely with Nancy.

"On the contrary," she said, "in order to rescue those kids we need the least number of people involved. The less noise we make, the less visible we are, the more successful we'll be."

Ned swung his head back, hurling a sigh in Eric's direction.

150

"For the decoy operation," Nancy said, "we can hold a big parade, send lots of people to attract attention. So long as Gutterman thinks that Dr. Bagley, Eric, you, and I are up there, he'll be completely fooled."

"I hope so," Ned said. "But why Eric? Why not me?"

Nancy walked over to him, laying her hand gently on his arm. Then, quietly and sweetly, enunciating each word, she said, "Because Eric can speak Hungarian, German, Czech, Russian, Polish, and even some Romanian. That's why."

Hesitating a moment, Ned smiled at Eric. "Hey, good luck. I do and don't envy you."

Eric merely smiled, allowing Dr. Bagley to resume questioning. "Well, we know who is going to try to bring the children out. I'd still like to know how."

"Oh, I forgot to tell you," Nancy said.

"Can you beat that?" Bess put in. "She forgot!"

"Gather round the map," the young detective said. "This," she went on, indicating a long body of water slightly pinched in the middle, "is a lake or *See* as the Austrians call it. It separates Hungary from Austria at this point, and the boundary line runs right through the middle. It is a popular resort area for the Austrians, though the Hungarian end of the lake is not so well developed and has miles of marshes and wetlands. This is the westernmost part of the famous steppe lakes that dot the Hungarian plain."

Nancy went on to explain that an oddity of this body of water, called the *Neusiedler See*, was its extreme shallowness, much like the lakes of Florida, with a depth averaging only four feet and with few points deeper than six feet.

"How did you find all of this out?" Ned asked.

"From an Austrian friend of my father's whom I called. He's well acquainted with the area and helped me make certain necessary arrangements there."

Nancy did not reveal what they were, however. "Anyway," she said, "we'll be able to slip into the water on the Austrian side, walk and wade south across the border, and come up on the shore within a few hundred yards of where the children and the Popovs are hiding. That's when we'll use the duck calls to communicate with them."

"That's fine," Professor Bagley said. "Ingenious, Nancy, really. But some of these children are only six years old. We don't know how many of them can swim. How—oh, of course, the inner tubes."

"That's right," Nancy said. "We'll blow them up in the water using the compressed-air tank, just before we cross the border."

"Why inner tubes?" Bess asked. "Why not the

kind of life jackets they have on airplanes?"

"Because they're bright yellow and it would be a job dying them black. Those jackets are made to be seen. Black inner tubes seemed to be the only answer for us. We'll lash them together and go wading and paddling into Hungary."

"Past the patrol boats. Past the mines. Past whatever protective barriers they may have put in the water," the professor stressed.

Nancy swallowed hard. "Well, we can't prepare for everything on such short notice. If there are boats, mines, barriers, we'll just have to pray we can dodge them and get through. There is always risk in everything that's worthwhile."

"I hate to throw more cold water on it," Dr. Bagley went on, "but one more question. How and where are you planning to go into the water? It stays light until about eleven o'clock in the evening this far north in August. Also, I seem to recall that the lakeshore is a resort area."

"So it's well populated," Ned added.

"That's right," the professor said. "You might have trouble slipping into the lake unnoticed. You'll probably have to cut through someone's property in order to get into the lake."

Nancy could hardly suppress her eagerness. "Oh, Dr. Bagley, I would love to tell you how we're going to make our entry into the water, but I can't. I want it to be a big surprise when we reconvene here at the hotel on Wednesday morning with all those children safe and sound."

"Can't you even give us a hint?" George asked.

"Well, I can say this. I will begin by arriving at the lake in a limousine with Eric posing as my chauffeur. I'll be wearing thick theatrical makeup and that gorgeous ball gown!"

The professor cast his eyes upward as Nancy threw her arms over her head, joyously watching the astonishment on her friends' faces.

"You're right, Nancy." Dr. Bagley chuckled. "It's better to keep it a secret. I don't think my heart could withstand another revelation."

18

A Hero Arrives

When Nancy arrived back at her room, she saw that the message light was blinking on her telephone. She called the front desk and the clerk promptly read her a cablegram from her father confirming that Kurt Kessler would arrive in Vienna that night via a connecting flight from London.

Nancy had barely enough time to phone Professor Bagley and arrange to drive with him to the airport and pick up the film director.

"You know, Dr. Bagley," Nancy said when they were finally on the way, "it's hard for me to remember any mystery I've ever worked on where I had so much responsibility for the lives of other people."

"I know how you feel," the professor replied. "I have very mixed feelings about meeting this ex-

tremely talented man. Tonight and tomorrow may
be his last free hours unless we succeed."

Despite their trepidations, both Nancy and Dr.
Bagley maintained happy expressions as they
watched the director cross the terminal from the
customs area.

"Mr. Kessler," Nancy said, walking toward him
with her hand outstretched, "I was sure I'd recog-
nize you right away."

The man smiled. "And I would know you anywhere, Miss Drew, since I have spent so many
hours in your father's office surrounded by your
photographs dating back to childhood days."

Nancy blushed crimson. "Oh," she said, "Mr.
Kessler, may I present Professor Bagley, the man
who was given the job of transferring the children
and who asked me to help."

As the director and the professor exchanged
greetings, Nancy studied Mr. Kessler's face. She
was saddened to see how very old he seemed.

Early newspaper photographs revealed him to
have been extremely handsome as a young man.
Now, though he was only middle-aged, his good
looks had been replaced by deep lines etched by
pain on weather-beaten skin. His eyes, which were
naturally deep-set, were even more sunken; and his
hair was grayish-white and quite thin.

He did all he could, however, to conceal his painful memories. He spoke with enthusiasm, and the soft, sad eyes were still capable of flashing with humor. As they walked back to the car, Nancy listened to his conversation with Dr. Bagley, thinking of Kurt Kessler weeping, when he was alone, for the things he had shown in *Captive Witness*.

I just have to find his film, she thought.

As the threesome rode back to the hotel, Nancy felt compelled to tell Mr. Kessler, "I'm the one who's guilty for getting you involved in all of this. If we fail to bring those children out and you are forced to go back across that border, I don't know what I'll—"

The director interrupted quickly. "No, Nancy. Never blame yourself. With or without you, the same things would have happened. The only difference now is I have you on my side."

"What bothers me," Dr. Bagley said, "is that even if we do manage to free the children, what's to prevent your enemies from trying to stop other people who want to leave and demanding you in exchange?"

"Look, anything is possible," Kessler replied, "but I think this is a single attempt. If they get me, they win; but if we get the orphans instead, there will be so much publicity that no one would dare trouble me again. By then, they will have been exposed and who would believe otherwise?"

"They want the world to see Kurt Kessler crossing the border voluntarily," the professor muttered.

"Of course," the director said. "They will probably have a crew there to film it, and with such a film, they can issue all kinds of propaganda—how the Americans forced me to make *Captive Witness,* how it is nothing but lies."

"So you don't think they intend to kidnap you?" Dr. Bagley asked.

Kessler shook his head. "No. Kidnapping me would serve no purpose. They want me to give up freely."

"It's so unfair and cruel," Nancy commented.

"On the contrary, Nancy," the film director said, "it's insane." Then his voice dropped. "What I dread most is that if I cross the border, I will find that my film has been destroyed."

He lapsed into a brooding silence which remained unbroken until the professor spoke.

"Mr. Kessler, I promise you that under the plan we've worked out there would be no way for them to get you across the frontier unless the film and the children are turned over."

"Besides," Nancy added, "we already know they don't have the orphans because just this evening we met Emile Popov, the man who is hiding them in Hungary."

Kurt Kessler sighed happily. "There are so many

exceptional people in this world. America has produced you and Dr. Bagley, and now you tell me about this Popov."

The discussion faded as the hotel came in sight. Nancy persuaded room service to serve a late snack in the professor's room where introductions were made to Eric and Mr. Popov. They excused themselves quickly and went to Ned's room next door, leaving the trio to talk alone for another hour. Nancy outlined the plan involving the decoy group and a strike team to accomplish the final mission.

"You are a marvel," Kessler said admiringly, "and if we all survive tomorrow, I am going to make a film about Nancy Drew."

The young detective floundered for an answer. "You may change your mind after you see me in action," she said, then realizing that wasn't quite what she meant, added quickly, "Of course, I do feel confident about—"

"I know you do," Mr. Kessler interposed gently, "and I am very grateful to you."

Without any further discussion, Nancy said good night and went to her room. At eleven the next morning, she heard a knock at the door. It was George wearing the titian wig, Nancy's dress, and the floppy straw hat. Standing right next to her was Ned. Their hands were clasped and they were gazing deeply into each other's eyes—or as deeply as they possibly could through their enormous sunglasses.

Nancy had to put her hand over her mouth to stifle her amusement. Then she hissed at him, "Stop that! You'll give us all away! Now scoot!"

Blowing kisses, Ned and George disappeared down the hall. Nancy went to the window, certain it was under surveillance, and peeked out to observe the rest of the decoy team stepping into the big rental car.

Burt, disguised as Eric, was being helped out of his wheelchair and into the front seat. Bess, Dave, and the professor were there, as was Kurt Kessler. Presently, Ned and George joined the group.

As their car pulled away, Nancy searched in vain for some sign of Gutterman's powder-blue car. It was nowhere in sight. A black Mercedes, however, containing two of the men she had seen skulking in the lobby, shot out from the curb and began shadowing the professors's vehicle.

Where was Gutterman, though? Nancy wondered.

Either he had already gone to Czechoslovakia and would greet the professor's team at the border, or he was lurking somewhere else.

What also vaguely worried her was how Gutterman expected to persuade Kessler into surrendering if Gutterman did not produce the children. Did he know where they were? Had he already swooped down on them in Hungary and transported them to the Czech border?

Nancy could imagine his cruel laughter as she and Eric plunged through the dark waters of the lake, sending out their duck-call signal in vain!

Then another chilling thought occurred to her. Suppose ten other children had been assembled at the Czech border, pretending that they were the orphans? Who would know the difference? Only Eric, whose thirteen-year-old cousin was among them, and Eric would be far away on the Hungarian frontier.

Oh, why didn't I ask Dr. Bagley if he had any way of confirming the children's identity? Nancy chided herself.

She puffed her cheeks and blew out the air in a great sigh of frustration. She had missed checking out one very important detail, so it would have to be left to fate!

Going to her dressing table, she opened the theatrical makeup kit and for the next hour, worked to transform herself from a fresh-faced young woman into a nineteenth-century lady at least ten years older, complete with a black beauty mark on her cheek.

Then she wriggled into the tight confines of the beautiful, glittering red ball gown. A glossy brunette wig with long, soft curls topped the disguise.

161

Although she wasn't sure if the wig style was typical of the late 1800s, she decided it complimented the outfit perfectly.

At four o'clock, Eric telephoned. "Your car awaits, madam," he said.

"Thank you, Otto," Nancy said. "I shall be down immediately."

Making no attempt to slip out quietly, Nancy swept down the main staircase into the lobby. Onlookers stared at her incredulously as she waltzed to the door where Eric, in a black wig and large black mustache, took her arm and led her to the rented limousine.

Nancy was completely aware that she had stepped past at least two of Gutterman's men but felt confident that they hadn't recognized her.

As the limousine drove off slowly, the assembled doorman, porters, guests, and passersby issued a round of applause. Nancy waved graciously.

"Who is that?" an American woman inquired upon entering the hotel.

"Oh," said the doorman, not wishing to appear ignorant of the hotel's guests, "she's a very famous actress. She stays here all the time."

All the way out of Vienna, Eric kept checking his rearview mirror to see if anyone was following them. Half an hour later, he said with a tone of caution, "I think we're in the clear, Nancy."

"I hope so, but keep an eye on that mirror. By the

way, Eric, you make a lovely chauffeur. And that mustache!"

"You like it?"

"It's beautiful."

"And may I compliment you, madam. You look wonderful. A little overdone for daytime perhaps, but so what?"

"Do you know the route by heart?" Nancy asked.

"Every inch including side roads. We are presently on Route 16 south. We will turn east on 304 through Eisenstadt. Then to Schützen, and after that I have to wind down some smaller roads until we reach Mörbisch."

"When we get there, I'll take over."

"I can't wait to find out why you are dressed that way." Eric laughed.

"You will—soon." Nancy giggled.

But their good humor was dampened when Eric, looking in his mirror, noticed a car following them. He alerted Nancy who, peering through her binoculars, picked up the powder-blue sedan with Gutterman and Burger inside.

"Ooh!" Nancy said in exasperation. "How—how? Gutterman seems so dumb sometimes but he isn't. He must have extrasensory perception or something close to it."

"I can try to lose them on a side road," Eric volunteered, frowning.

"No, we'd only wind up in trouble for breaking the speed limit. Do me a favor, though. Pull into the next service area and look for a spot where we can't be observed too easily."

Within a few minutes, Eric found the right place and brought the big limousine to a halt. Gutterman and Burger drove by trying to appear disinterested.

"Doesn't he realize we'd spot that blue car a mile away?" Nancy muttered. "I don't understand that man at all."

Hurriedly, they bought several cans of motor oil. Nancy climbed into the trunk, carefully protecting her voluminous dress. Eric propped the trunk lid so that it stayed open about eight inches and handed Nancy the oilcans and an opener.

They soon overtook Gutterman and Burger who had pulled over to wait at a roadside stand. As soon as the limousine went past, the evil duo started trailing them again. Nancy, feeling the car round a big bend, punched holes in two of the cans and began pouring the oil on the road. She quickly opened two more cans and repeated the process.

Gutterman and Burger, who were several hundred yards to the rear, could not see this until it was too late. As their car hit the slippery fluid, it went into a long skid, sending it off the road, down a ravine, and into a swamp where it settled in mud.

Eric stopped the limousine at a stand, and quickly notified the police of an oil slick so that other motorists would be alerted. Then, with Nancy rejoining him, they resumed their ride.

"Gutterman will be steaming now," the young detective said, her blue eyes dancing, "but I had no choice."

Inwardly, though, she was beginning to worry. Gutterman had probably guessed where she was going. He must have known she was heading for the outdoor theater on the lake at Mörbisch. Otherwise, why would she be wearing theatrical attire?

Nancy now revealed her complete plan to Eric. She would join the chorus in *The Merry Widow*, an operetta being performed at Mörbisch. The theater was one of Austria's most popular tourist attractions. Since Nancy had played in the Footlighters' production of the same operetta, she was capable of singing the entire score. She had arranged to become a member of the Mörbisch chorus for one night only.

"But what does all this have to do with rescuing ten children?" Eric questioned.

"Everything," Nancy said. "Remember, the professor said we might have trouble getting into the water without being seen? Well, the theater is built out over the lake. When the show finishes, the sun will have set and we'll be able to slip into the water behind the building, inflate our inner tubes, and sail for Hungary."

166

Eric whistled in admiration. "What an idea! Pure genius!"

"I wouldn't go that far." Nancy grinned as they pulled up to the theater.

"Tell me, how did you manage to talk your way into the theatrical company?"

"That was easy," Nancy said, shaking her brown wig. "Oh, and there's the man who worked me into the company. Let me introduce you."

Nancy rushed toward him, hugging the tall, white-haired man as he stood in front. His name was Georg Waldheim, a dear friend of her father's. He was a patron of the arts, and knew many people connected with the theater, so it was simple enough for him to gain permission for Nancy to sing.

Saying good-bye to Herr Waldheim, who whispered good luck to her in her mission, Nancy led Eric backstage. He was carrying the suitcase filled with the inner tubes, the small air tank, and the rubber suits. Eric was to remain there throughout the performance. He sat quietly, waiting for the dressing rooms to empty, then scurried out a window and climbed down on the pilings with the suitcase. He set up camp where no one could see him sitting on the wooden supports.

Nancy went onstage and sang her heart out as night began to fall. Eric, meanwhile, inflated the tubes, donned his rubber suit, and applied black greasepaint to his skin in order to stay better hidden in the dark.

But toward the end of the last act, as Nancy was caught up in the swell of lush melodies, she happened to glance out into the audience. There with his opera glasses trained on the performers was Herr Gutterman!

19

Across the Frontier

The girl detective had to conquer the urge to crouch down or hide behind the other singers. Any movement she made would make her stand out immediately, and Gutterman would be sure to identify her.

So, instead, she continued to sing to the very last note. But the minute the lights were dimmed for curtain calls, she broke out of the line and raced toward the dressing rooms. Quickly, she wriggled out of her dress into her bathing attire, and again slipped the gown over her head.

Before the rest of the cast had left the stage, Nancy was out a side door and approaching the water. It was almost as dark as the night itself, and not until she reached the protective shadows of the trees did she dare to remove the dress covering her scuba suit.

She joined Eric on the pilings where the inflated inner tubes lay lashed together with cord. Nancy covered her hands and face with the remaining greasepaint and waited with Eric for the cast and crew to leave the theater.

Above them they could hear conversation mixed with laughter and footsteps. Then a voice cut through the noise. "Nancy Drew! Has anyone seen her? I have an urgent message for her."

Nancy and Eric exchanged glances. "I know it's Gutterman. He has an uncanny ability to alter his voice and appearance, but I'm positive it's he."

Her companion nodded as the voice called out again.

"What does he expect me to do? Rush right out and say 'Here I am'?" Nancy said.

"More likely, he's hoping somebody else will spot you and say 'There she is!' " Eric replied. "On the other hand, what if Dr. Bagley is trying to reach us?"

"No chance," Nancy said brightly.

"Why not?"

"Because he doesn't know where we are, remember?"

Eric grinned. "You're right."

"I only kept this part of the plan a secret to surprise everybody later. Now it's working to our advantage."

Although it seemed like hours, probably no more than twenty minutes passed until everyone had left and the theater lights were extinguished. There was silence except for the night sounds of the lake and the chirping and shrill of insects and night birds. Then Eric groaned.

"What's the matter, Eric?"

"The car. It's still there. I left it in plain sight. Gutterman will see it. He knows we drove down in a limousine so he'll know you're still in the area."

"And he'll go right to the closest Hungarian border crossing and alert the guards. The whole frontier force will be onto us!" Nancy cried. "We have to move fast!"

Slipping into the water and pushing the raft of inner tubes ahead of them, they began moving south as fast as they could without making splashing sounds.

"I can't see you," Nancy whispered back. "Everything is black on black."

"Maybe we should hold hands," the young man suggested.

"Well," Nancy said, smiling to herself, "we can always hang onto the string of tubes. As long as we don't lose them, we'll always be together."

It was Eric's turn to smile, his white teeth gleaming in the night. "We could," he said, "but it'd be nicer the other way."

"Eric," Nancy said, "no offense but you'll have to keep your mouth closed because your beautiful white teeth shine like a beacon."

He chuckled. "Okay, let's go. No more small talk."

Half wading and half swimming, they made good time. Nancy estimated their speed at about one and a half miles per hour or, roughly speaking, half the speed of walking. Therefore, it would take them approximately an hour to reach the point where they expected to find the Popovs and the children.

Occasionally, they stumbled into holes but soon learned to glide with their feet just grazing the bottom.

The shoreline became increasingly swamplike as they moved into Hungarian territory, and there were few lights to show them where land was. Since it was now close to midnight, most house lights had been extinguished. For a while, the two young people lost their bearings and were forced to stop.

"What I wouldn't give for one burst of moonlight," Nancy said.

She had no sooner spoken when a tremendous flash of light zigzagged across the sky followed by a clap of thunder. In the glow that spread over the whole lake, they could see clearly that they weren't far from the twisted tree that Popov had said was near his hiding place.

"Are you all right, Nancy?" Eric asked.

"Yes, but scared. I thought they were shooting artillery at us."

"Give them the signal," Eric went on.

Taking out her duck call, Nancy blew three short, sharp quacks. There was no answer. She tried again, but still no reply.

"Should we go up onshore?" Eric asked.

Nancy was about to say yes when they heard the answering cry of Popov's duck call. Moments later, faint shadows bulked out of the night and Nancy and Eric waded ashore to meet them.

Emile Popov was carrying one child, a six-year-old. "He can sleep through anything," he said, handing the boy to Eric. "Be careful when you put him in the tube. The water will wake him and we don't want him to cry out."

Nancy and Mrs. Popov took the other two six-year-olds. The older children gathered around Emile Popov, holding onto a rope he carried to keep them together.

Eric began speaking softly to the children, paying special attention to the thirteen-year-old boy who was his cousin. In spite of their joyous reunion, the two kept their voices low.

Nancy now took charge of painting everyone's

faces black, but as she finished, Eric whispered nervously.

"Listen! Everyone be still."

The group froze at the sound of several automobiles approaching.

"Trouble," Mr. Popov said. "They're coming. No one else would be coming at this hour. Quickly! Quickly!"

Shoving off and keeping low behind the high reeds that covered the inshore waters, the little convoy began moving north again toward the Austrian border.

Car doors opened and closed now and the loud voices of Hungarian police guards drifted across the lake. They trained their flashlights on the hut where the refugees had hidden, then swung the lights toward the shore.

Did they suspect that the escape was being made by water? Would they send out boats? Nancy knew that the Hungarians had small patrol craft as did the Austrians, but since this was a relatively peaceful border, she hadn't worried about them.

The urgency of the situation prompted all of the children, except the smallest, to slip out of the tubes and help push. Each of the older ones stayed close to a younger one, using a buddy system they had devised over months of hiding throughout Eastern Europe.

The searchers, running now along the shore, shone their lights out across the water.

"Stop," Nancy whispered.

Everyone halted instantly. The flashlight beams played over and around them, but the darkness of their attire and the cover of tall reeds kept them from being seen.

If only it would rain to block their vision, Nancy thought.

But the rain didn't come and the flashlights continued to sweep across the lake. Then, after ten minutes, drops began to dot the water. Within another minute, a full-scale storm was raging, and the curtains of water made the flashlights useless.

Jubilantly, the convoy started moving again. Pushing and swimming as hard as they could, they approached the Austrian border. The flashlights, now dim blobs, receded toward the direction from which they had come.

"Only two hundred yards to go," Eric whispered over his shoulder.

"Look!" Nancy exclaimed suddenly.

Lying directly in front of them was a powerful light that attempted to cut through the heavy rain. It was mounted on a small patrol boat.

For the first time since their mission began, Nancy wanted to cry. There was no way to tell if it was a Hungarian or Austrian craft in the dark. They were so close to freedom, and the children were so cold from the lake water that they struggled to keep their teeth from chattering.

Oh, please help us, Nancy prayed as Eric moved to her side.

"I've got an idea," he whispered. "I'm going to swim out toward the center of the lake, a few hundred yards or so, then cross to the Austrian side. Then I'll start shouting and screaming like a maniac. The patrol is sure to be distracted enough so you can scoot through with the kids."

"Oh, Eric, am I glad you dreamed that one up. I just ran out of ideas. Be careful, though."

"I will."

It took the young man fifteen minutes to position himself. By then, the rain had slackened and the light from the boat was scanning the area with such intensity that the little group was forced to wade far back into the reeds and crouch low.

Suddenly, Nancy heard Eric. He was whooping and yelling like an Indian tribal attack on a frontier fort. The men in the patrol boat reacted instantly and cruised toward the uproar.

Pushing out of the reeds once again, Nancy and the Popovs covered the final distance of the border in five minutes. They didn't stop until they reached the theater. Coming out of the water into the chill night air, some of the children at last began to whimper. The Popovs went from one to the other, murmuring words of comfort for they were now safe on Austrian soil.

While the couple led the children to the limousine where warm blankets awaited them, Nancy observed an Austrian patrol boat pull ashore with Eric and two Austrian policeman. They wanted to see for themselves if the young man's tale about the refugees was true. Discovering that it was, they saluted and left.

Of course, jamming so many people into one automobile, even though it was large and ten of the occupants small, was no easy task. But nothing could dampen anyone's spirits. Within half an hour, most of the children had fallen asleep. Nancy was surrounded by four of the smallest ones in the front seat.

"Are you happy, Eric?" she asked.

"It's a dream come true," he said, "and may I add that you were fantastic."

"Oh, I don't know about that," she said with a lilt in her voice. "You're the one who really wins the honors. If you hadn't pulled that stunt, we never would have made it."

"Aw, shucks," Eric said, imitating the twang of Old West movie heroes. "It weren't nothin'."

Nancy laughed, but a sobering thought stopped her. Everything except recovering Kurt Kessler's film had been accomplished. He had risked his life to help save the children, but the young detective's personal assignment to find *Captive Witness* had failed.

For the rest of the trip back to the hotel, she racked her brain. Was there no way to recover that film?

20

Herr Gutterman Unmasked

When they finally reached the hotel, the Popovs and the children were met by members of the refugee organization. It would arrange their transportation to relatives and friends in England and America.

Professor Bagley then related the events at the Czechoslovakian border. "They tried to fool us by showing up with ten other children who had been trained to lie about their identities. Fortunately, I had been given photographs of the real orphans. How the Hungarians carried on, screaming and threatening!"

"George took off her wig and waved it at them." Bess giggled. "That really infuriated them."

"Then Burt got out of the wheelchair and started dancing with her." Dave laughed. "The commissar or whoever he was turned purple!"

"On the whole, it has been a huge success." Dr. Bagley smiled. "Thanks largely to Nancy."

"You are much too kind, sir," she said. "Everyone did his or her part beautifully. The only thing that has me down is the fact I can't find *Captive Witness*.

Kurt Kessler, who was enjoying a cup of coffee and chatting with Ned, turned to reassure Nancy again. "Yes, I wish I had my film back, but I'll make other films—better ones, too. Please don't worry so."

Nancy explained, though, that it was irritating to have seen half of it yet to be unable to locate the place where it had been shown.

"You actually saw it?" the director cried, causing Nancy to reveal the incident of her meeting with Gutterman.

"Unfortunately, Vienna has no grid system of streets like other cities," Nancy said, "so the twists and turns we took really confused me." She paused a second. "I did hear certain sounds, though."

"What were they?" Kurt Kessler inquired with mounting eagerness.

"Well, trains. A train yard, to be exact, and a merry-go-round."

The film director furrowed his brow for a few moments, absentmindedly pulling at his shirt cuffs. Suddenly, he stopped and gripped the table with both hands. "Wait a minute!" he exclaimed. "I stayed in Vienna for a time before going to America, and I think I know where you were."

Nancy and the director dashed down the three flights of stairs, found the rental car and, with Mr. Kessler at the wheel, they headed north.

"You were somewhere between the great railroad yards up ahead and the Prater amusement park on the right. The building with its twelve steps has to be around here."

Completely elated, Nancy shone her flashlight on the buildings as her companion drove the car up and down the streets in the area. They found nothing, though.

"Let's not give up yet," Nancy said, causing him to speed the vehicle in another direction. Silently, they rode down a series of side streets lined with more old, run-down buildings. Then Kurt Kessler turned a sharp corner, and Nancy gasped in excitement. "There—down that side street. The second building! It has twelve steps!"

Kessler counted them and accelerated the gas pedal. When he finally halted the car, they stepped out fast and hurried up to the front door. It was locked, but it took the director only a few seconds to open the lock with a tiny metal pick.

"Someday I'll have to tell you how I escaped out of Hungary," he said to Nancy who was grinning almost as broadly as he was.

Once inside, the young detective closed her eyes, recalling how she had been turned when taken there by Gutterman. She indicated the door to the director. He motioned her to stand back as he listened carefully.

"Someone is in there," he said softly. Then, without another word, he put his shoulder to the door and burst through. Nancy was right on his heels.

"Good evening," came a voice from a chair that swiveled to face the two visitors.

It was Adolph Gutterman! In one hand, he was holding the film *Captive Witness* and in the other, a flaming cigarette lighter. His eyes seemed glazed as if he were entranced by the fire.

Kessler moved forward, slowly, staring into them. "Hagedorn?" he said softly. "Heinrich Hagedorn?"

Gutterman did not reply. The lighter was flaming wildly now, threatening to singe the man's finger. Gently, Kessler took the lighter and then the film. He placed it in its tin container.

"You know him?" Nancy asked in bewilderment, adding, "I don't understand—he just let you take the film right out of his hand without a protest."

Kessler lowered his eyes toward Hagedorn's trembling fingers as they covered his face, muffling a deep cry.

"We were in the film business together when we were young," Kessler murmured. "He was a good director. A great actor. A master of disguises, voice changes. One of the best in the world."

"How did he come to be a spy then?" Nancy asked.

As she spoke, the man slumped back in his chair, frozen in shock.

"It's a long story," the director continued. "I don't even know it all. He lost both parents in Nazi concentration camps. Those who took control, fed him, educated him, trained him to act and direct. But he was too wild, too creative. He wanted to do things his own way.

"He made a short film that was the most devastating attack on political oppression I have ever seen."

"More devastating than *Captive Witness?*" Nancy asked.

"Much more. He went to prison for years because of it. Then suddenly, he was released on condition that he make propaganda films for his country. What he really was being trained for was a future in espionage. He became a spy in order to keep his wife and children fed."

Now Kessler's voice began to waver. "He had

183

compromised everything for the people he cared about most—"

"I still don't understand, though, why he just let you take that film right out of his hand," Nancy interrupted quietly.

Kessler took a deep breath before going on. "Because of our friendship, I suppose," he said.

"He and I were in prison at the same time. When he finally managed to get out, he helped me escape. I remember he said it was more important for my film work to be seen than his.

"Unfortunately, neither Heinrich nor I realized that our captors would pin my escape on him. The next thing I learned was that his wife and children had been killed in an automobile accident."

"How terrible!" Nancy gasped.

She gazed at the man in the chair whose eyes were now pinched shut. No wonder he had behaved so erratically, appearing brilliant one moment and childlike another. He was only playing the role of someone who wouldn't permit himself to be hurt again. Seeing Kurt Kessler, however, had revived those feelings he had attempted, perhaps unsuccessfully, to abandon.

After Kessler had placed a call to the police, Nancy told him thoughtfully, "I've learned a lot from this experience, mostly that you can't understand what other people have to endure unless you put yourself in their shoes."

Of course, she had no idea that she would soon face another, similar challenge when she solved *The Gondolier's Secret*.

"That's why I make movies," the film director said. "I made *Captive Witness* to show the world how the other half is forced to live."

Nancy's eyes flashed to the tin container Kessler had held tightly since he took it from his old friend. "And I guarantee that everyone who sees this picture will be a captive audience!" she exclaimed.

A few days later, when the young detective and her traveling companions were gathered at the Vienna Film Festival awards ceremony, they listened intently to the names of those recommended as producer of the Best Foreign Documentary. Kurt Kessler was one of five nominees, all of whom had done outstanding film work.

"I'll be so disappointed if he doesn't win," Bess confided to Nancy as someone on stage opened an envelope.

Kessler, who sat on the other side of the girl, murmured under his breath during the endless wait, then gasped as his name was called. A huge round of applause went up from the audience.

"Oh, I'm so happy for you," Nancy told him, letting him step quickly into the aisle.

When he reached the microphone, everyone was still clapping loudly and he quieted them with his hands. "Please, please. You are all too kind," he said. "I cannot accept this award alone. I must share it with someone without whose courageous help I would not be standing here now."

A murmur rose among his listeners, as he paused before going on. "Nancy Drew, will you please join me here?"

"Me?" Nancy said quietly.

"Yes, you!" her other friends whispered from behind, coaxing her out of her seat. "You deserve it, Nancy!"

NANCY DREW MYSTERY STORIES®
by Carolyn Keene

You will also enjoy

THE LINDA CRAIG® SERIES
by Ann Sheldon